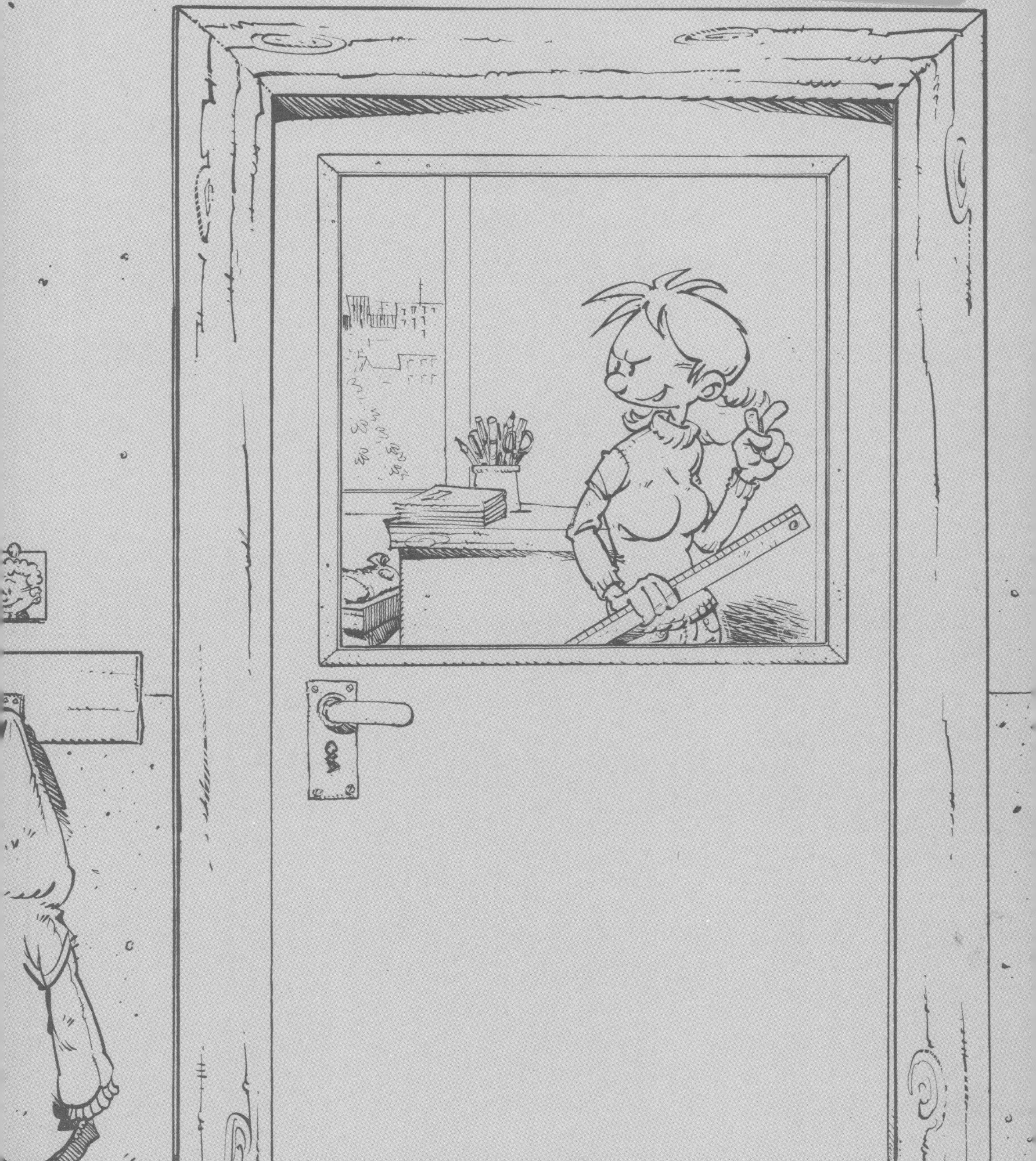

Thierry Coppée • Story and Art
Lorien • Color

PAPERCUTZ™
New York

Thanks to Valérie for the provisions.
Thanks to Théo, Julien, and Antonin for their encouragement.
To my friends.
To Jean Roba for the reading pleasures he gave me during my childhood.

A thousand thanks to my little family for everything and even more.

To the children who are gone too soon and to parents who depart too quickly.

Th. C.

A thousand kisses to my darling.
A thousand million smooches to my little Méloïse
and billions of blistering blue barnacles!

L.

TOTO TROUBLE Graphic Novels Available from Papercutz

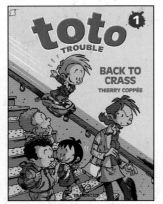

Graphic Novel #1
"Back to Crass"

Graphic Novel #2
"A Deadly Jokester"

Graphic Novel #3
"The Ace of Jokers"

TOTO TROUBLE graphic novels are available for $7.99 in paperback, and $12.99 in hardcover. Available from booksellers everywhere. You can also order online from papercutz.com. Or call 1-800-886-1223, Monday through Friday, 9 – 5 EST. MC, Visa, and AmEx accepted. To order by mail, please add $4.00 for postage and handling for first book ordered, $1.00 for each additional book, and make check payable to NBM Publishing. Send to: Papercutz, 160 Broadway, Suite 700, East Wing, New York, NY 10038.

papercutz.com

TOTO TROUBLE #3 "The Ace of Jokers"
Les Blagues de Toto, volumes 5-6, Coppée
© Éditions Delcourt, 2007-2008

Thierry Coppée – Writer & Artist
Lorien – Colorist
Joe Johnson – Translation
Tom Orzechowski – Lettering
Jeff Whitman – Production Coordinator
Michael Petranek – Editor
Jim Salicrup
Editor-in-Chief

ISBN: 978-1-62991-177-9 paperback edition
ISBN: 978-1-62991-178-6 hardcover edition

Printed in China
April 2015 by O.G. Printing Productions, LTD.
Units 2&3, 5/F, Lemmi Centre
50 Hoi Yuen Road, Kwon Tong, Kowloon

Papercutz books may be purchased for business or promotional use. For information on bulk purchases please contact Macmillan Corporate and Premium Sales Department at (800) 221-7945 x5442.

Distributed by Macmillan
First Papercutz Printing

Signs of the Times

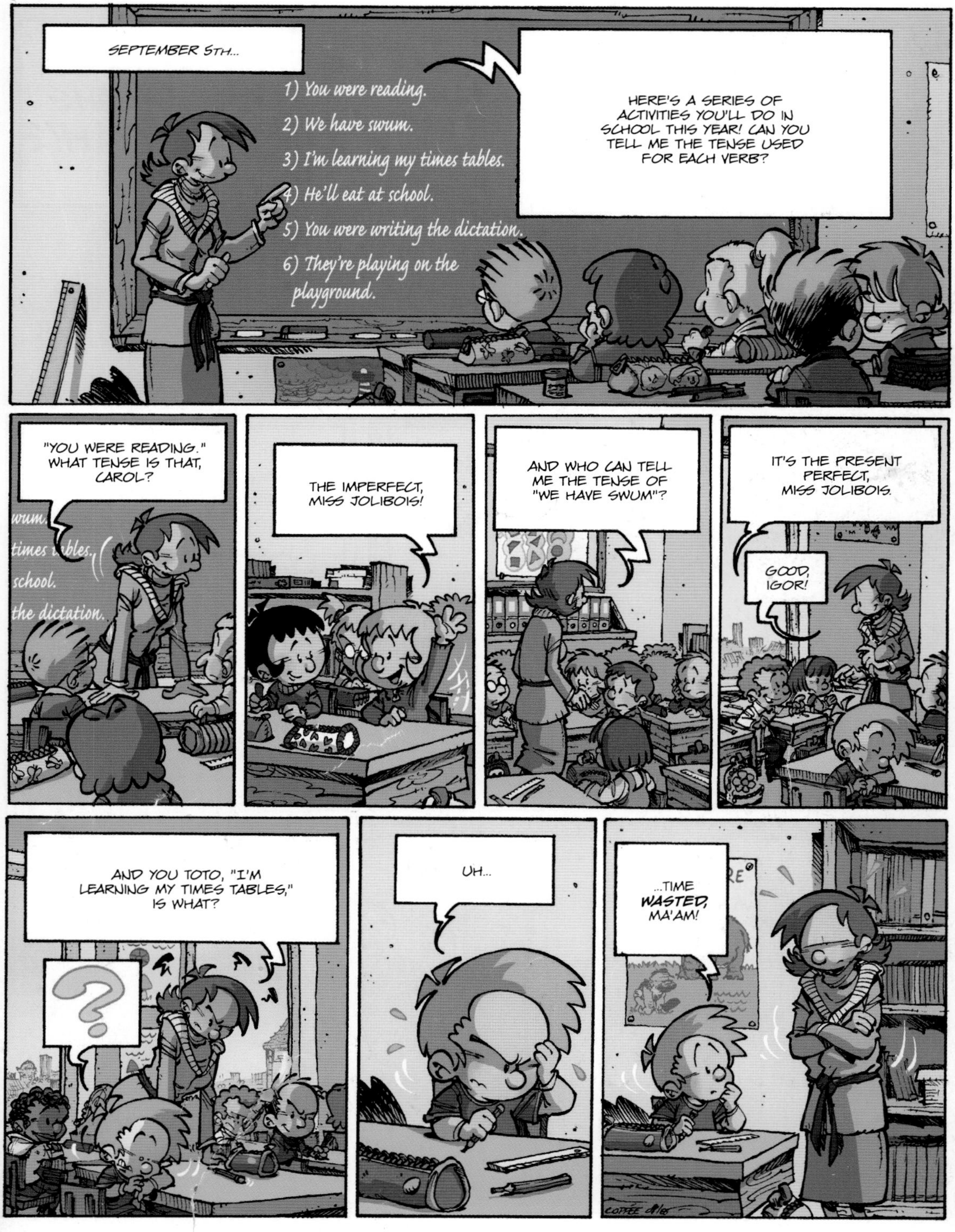

SEPTEMBER 5TH...
1) You were reading.
2) We have swum.
3) I'm learning my times tables.
4) He'll eat at school.
5) You were writing the dictation.
6) They're playing on the playground.
HERE'S A SERIES OF ACTIVITIES YOU'LL DO IN SCHOOL THIS YEAR! CAN YOU TELL ME THE TENSE USED FOR EACH VERB?
"YOU WERE READING." WHAT TENSE IS THAT, CAROL?
THE IMPERFECT, MISS JOLIBOIS!
AND WHO CAN TELL ME THE TENSE OF "WE HAVE SWUM"?
IT'S THE PRESENT PERFECT, MISS JOLIBOIS.
GOOD, IGOR!
AND YOU TOTO, "I'M LEARNING MY TIMES TABLES," IS WHAT?
?
UH...
...TIME WASTED, MA'AM!

The Proof is in the Pudding

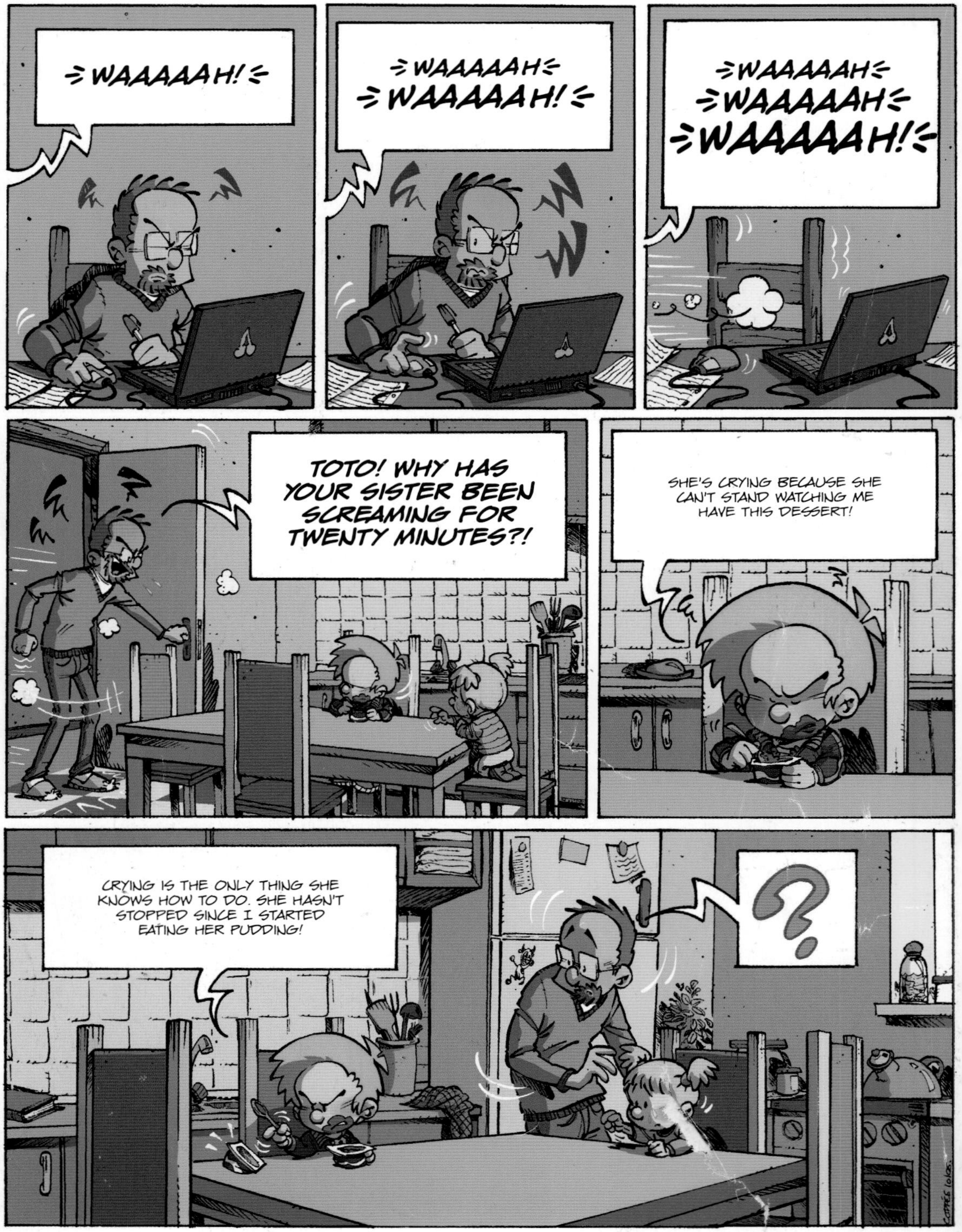

WAAAAAH!
WAAAAAH
WAAAAAH!
WAAAAAH
WAAAAAH
WAAAAAH!
TOTO! WHY HAS YOUR SISTER BEEN SCREAMING FOR TWENTY MINUTES?!
SHE'S CRYING BECAUSE SHE CAN'T STAND WATCHING ME HAVE THIS DESSERT!
CRYING IS THE ONLY THING SHE KNOWS HOW TO DO. SHE HASN'T STOPPED SINCE I STARTED EATING HER PUDDING!
?

Arbor Day

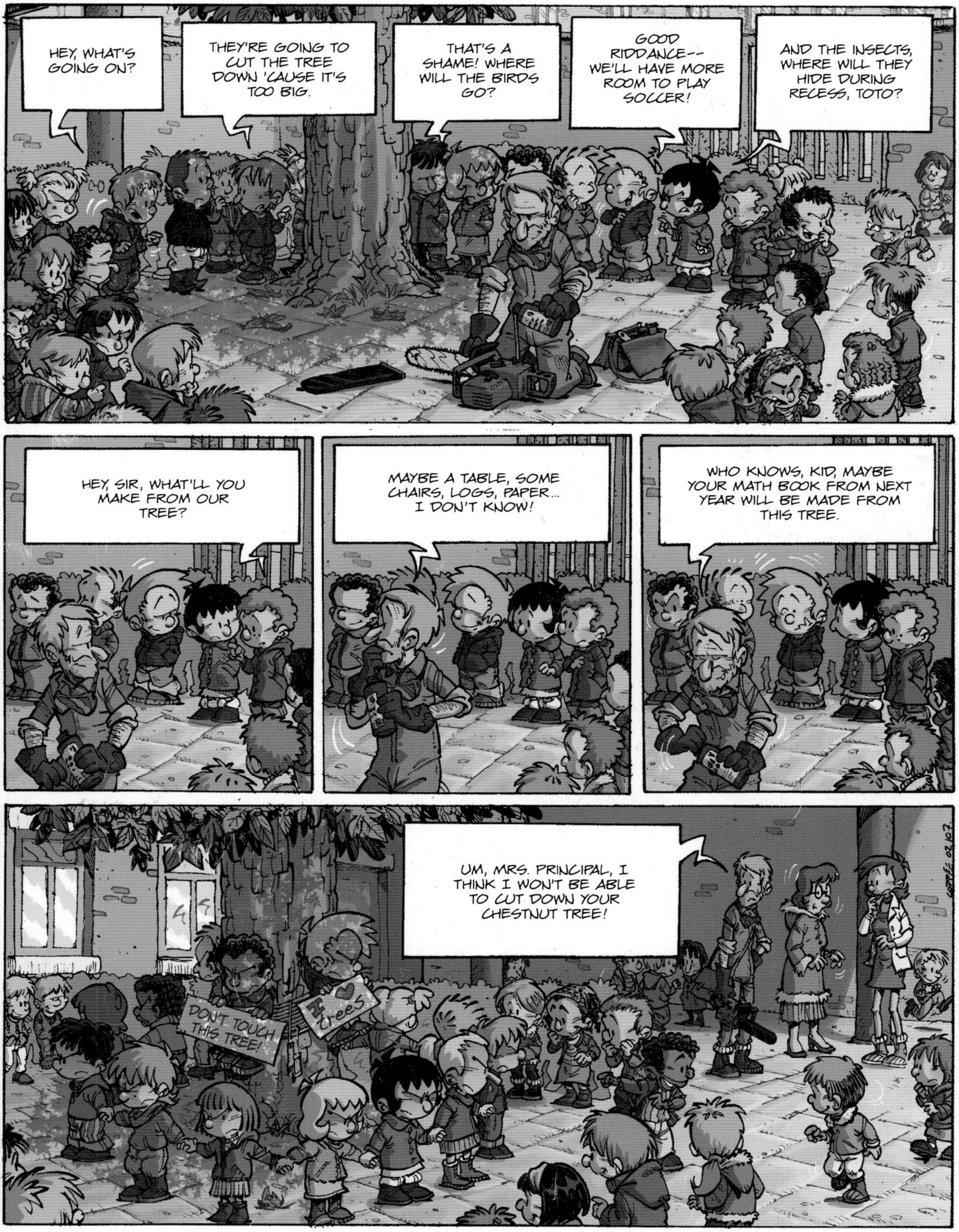
HEY, WHAT'S GOING ON?
THEY'RE GOING TO CUT THE TREE DOWN 'CAUSE IT'S TOO BIG.
THAT'S A SHAME! WHERE WILL THE BIRDS GO?
GOOD RIDDANCE-- WE'LL HAVE MORE ROOM TO PLAY SOCCER!
AND THE INSECTS, WHERE WILL THEY HIDE DURING RECESS, TOTO?
HEY, SIR, WHAT'LL YOU MAKE FROM OUR TREE?
MAYBE A TABLE, SOME CHAIRS, LOGS, PAPER... I DON'T KNOW!
WHO KNOWS, KID, MAYBE YOUR MATH BOOK FROM NEXT YEAR WILL BE MADE FROM THIS TREE.
DON'T TOUCH THIS TREE!
UM, MRS. PRINCIPAL, I THINK I WON'T BE ABLE TO CUT DOWN YOUR CHESTNUT TREE!

Profits and Losses

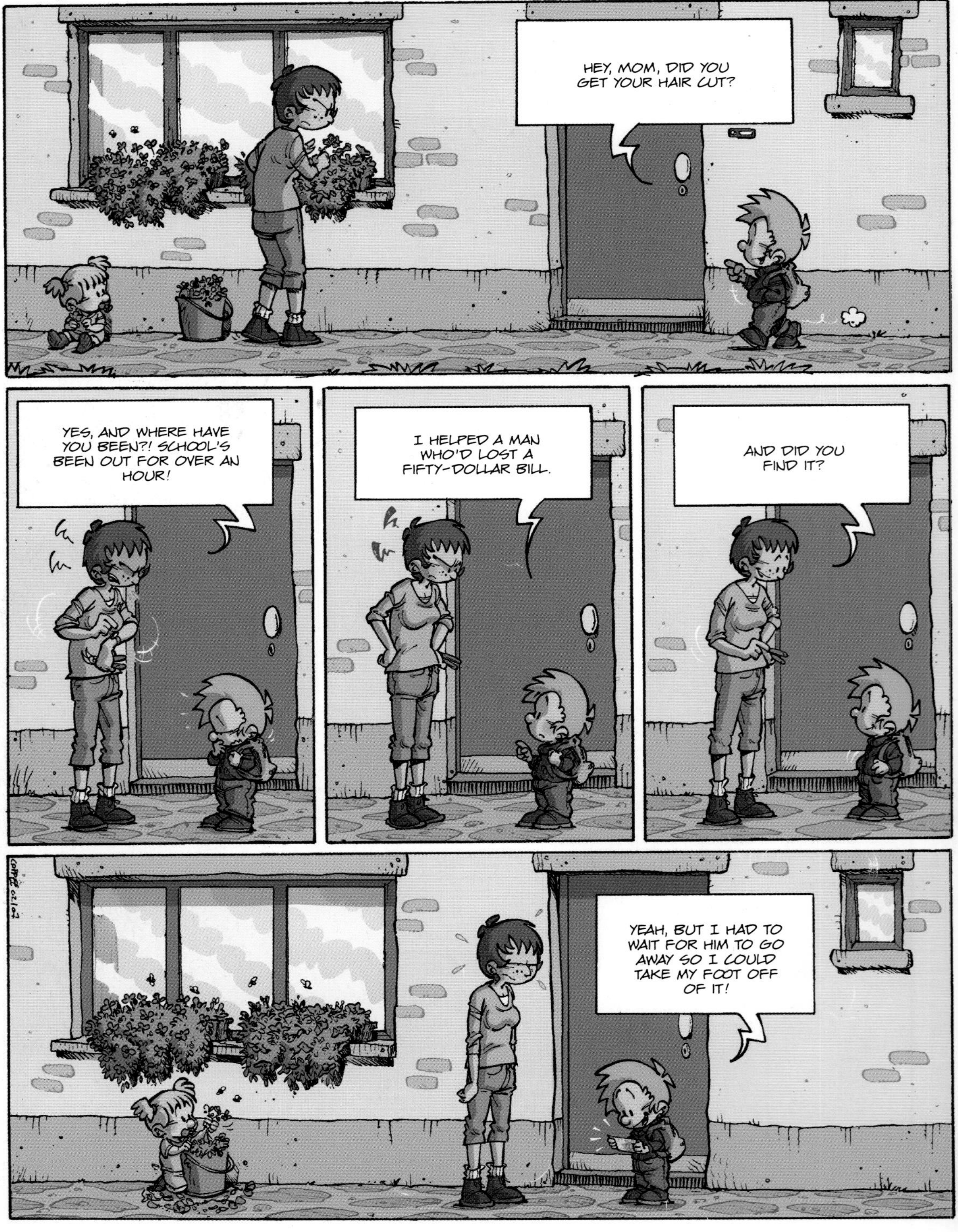
HEY, MOM, DID YOU GET YOUR HAIR CUT?
YES, AND WHERE HAVE YOU BEEN?! SCHOOL'S BEEN OUT FOR OVER AN HOUR!
I HELPED A MAN WHO'D LOST A FIFTY-DOLLAR BILL.
AND DID YOU FIND IT?
YEAH, BUT I HAD TO WAIT FOR HIM TO GO AWAY SO I COULD TAKE MY FOOT OFF OF IT!

The Verb of the Day

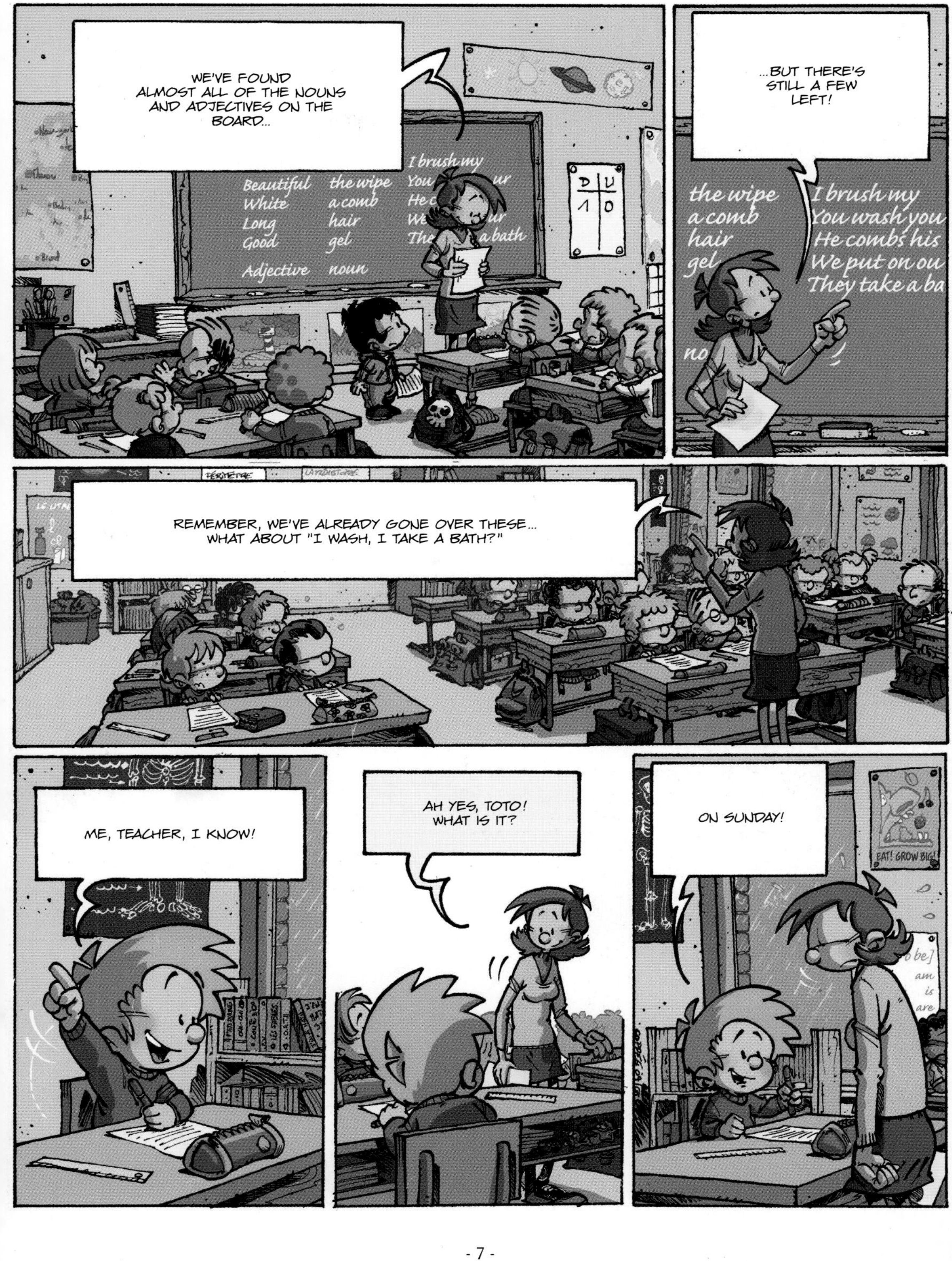

WE'VE FOUND ALMOST ALL OF THE NOUNS AND ADJECTIVES ON THE BOARD...
...BUT THERE'S STILL A FEW LEFT!
REMEMBER, WE'VE ALREADY GONE OVER THESE... WHAT ABOUT "I WASH, I TAKE A BATH?"
ME, TEACHER, I KNOW!
AH YES, TOTO! WHAT IS IT?
ON SUNDAY!

The Old Rifle

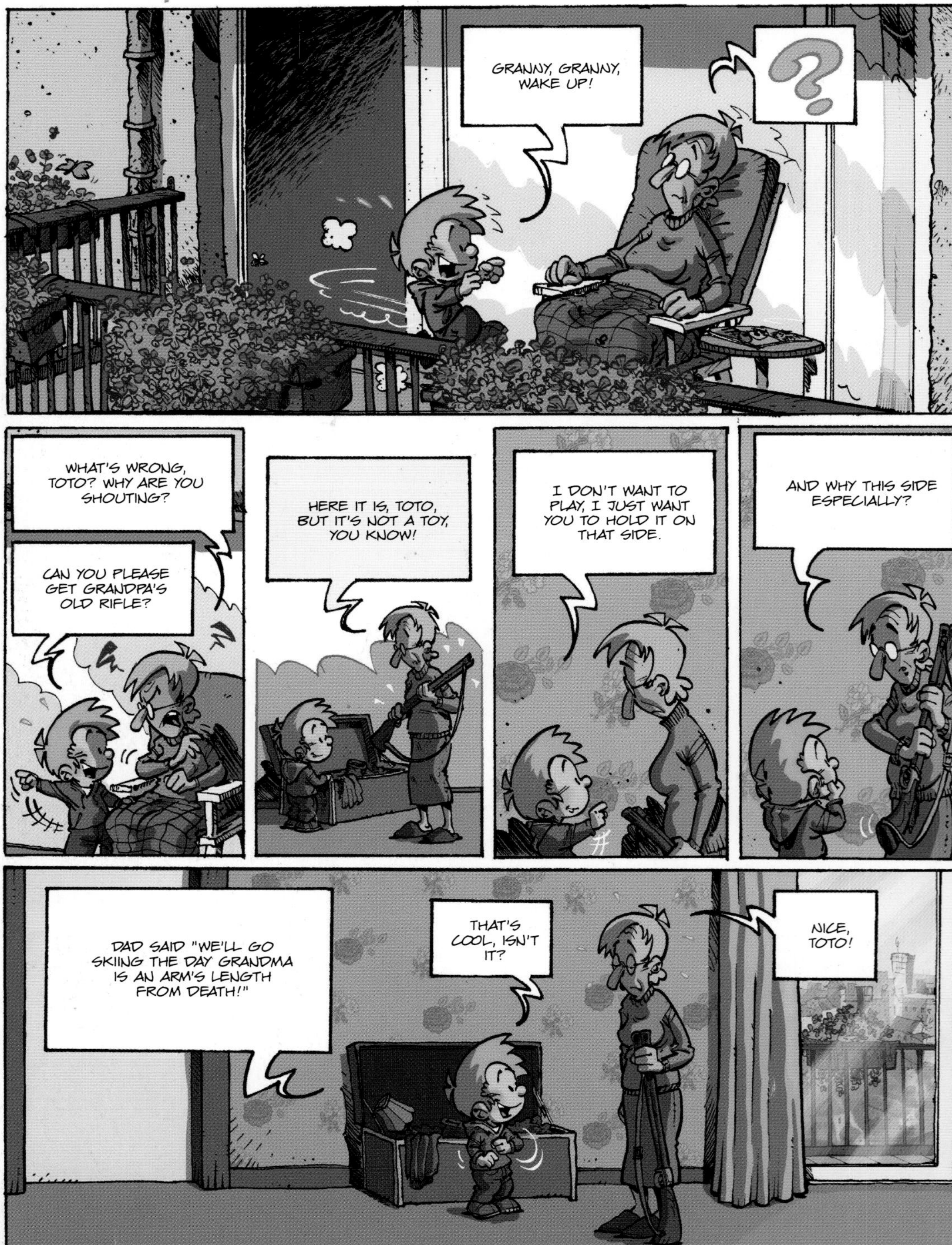
GRANNY, GRANNY, WAKE UP!
?
WHAT'S WRONG, TOTO? WHY ARE YOU SHOUTING?
CAN YOU PLEASE GET GRANDPA'S OLD RIFLE?
HERE IT IS, TOTO, BUT IT'S NOT A TOY, YOU KNOW!
I DON'T WANT TO PLAY, I JUST WANT YOU TO HOLD IT ON THAT SIDE.
AND WHY THIS SIDE ESPECIALLY?
DAD SAID "WE'LL GO SKIING THE DAY GRANDMA IS AN ARM'S LENGTH FROM DEATH!"
THAT'S COOL, ISN'T IT?
NICE, TOTO!
COPPÉE 10/05.

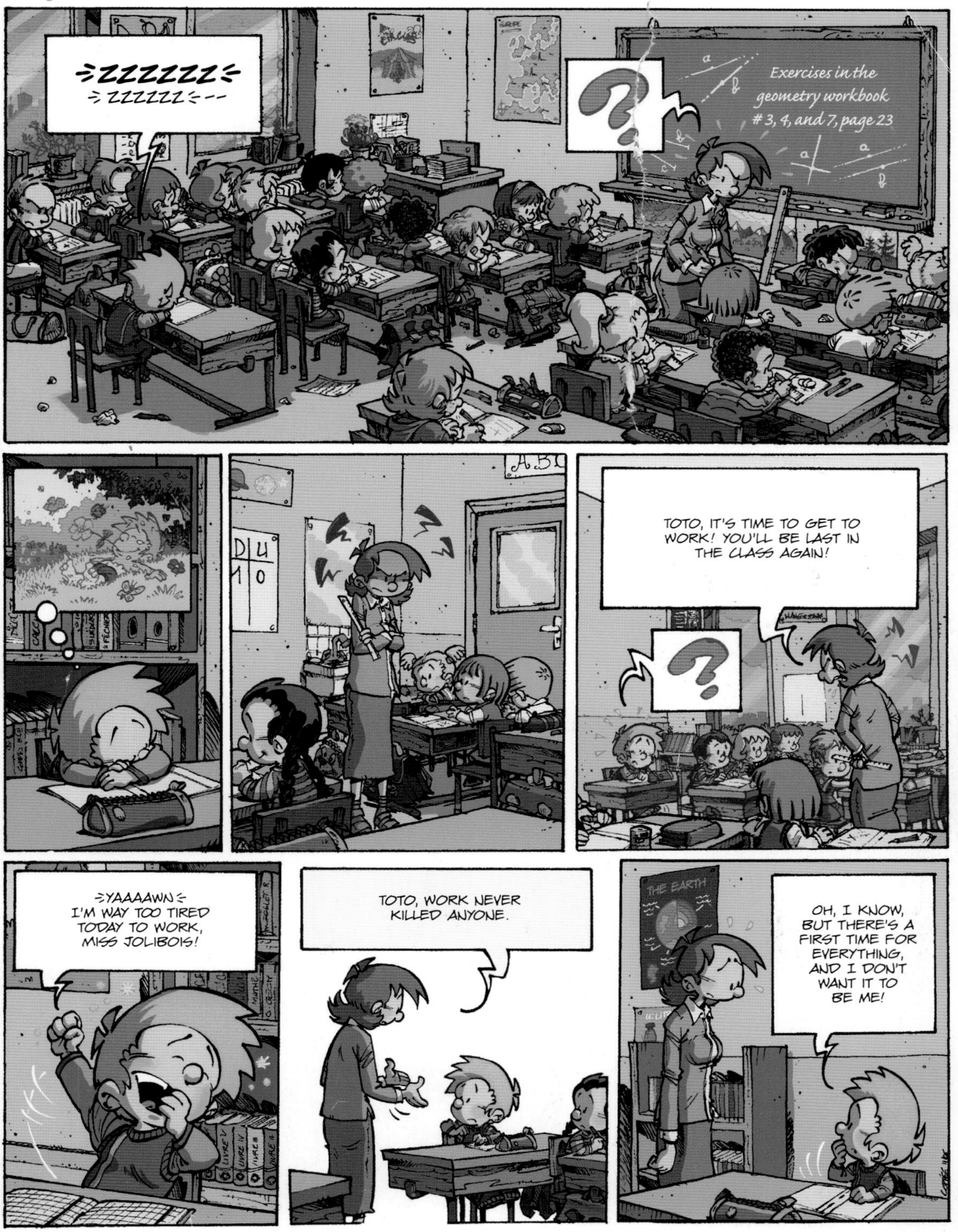

ZZZZZZ
ZZZZZZ
?
Exercises in the geometry workbook # 3, 4, and 7, page 23
D U
1 0
TOTO, IT'S TIME TO GET TO WORK! YOU'LL BE LAST IN THE CLASS AGAIN!
?
YAAAAWN
I'M WAY TOO TIRED TODAY TO WORK, MISS JOLIBOIS!
TOTO, WORK NEVER KILLED ANYONE.
THE EARTH
OH, I KNOW, BUT THERE'S A FIRST TIME FOR EVERYTHING, AND I DON'T WANT IT TO BE ME!

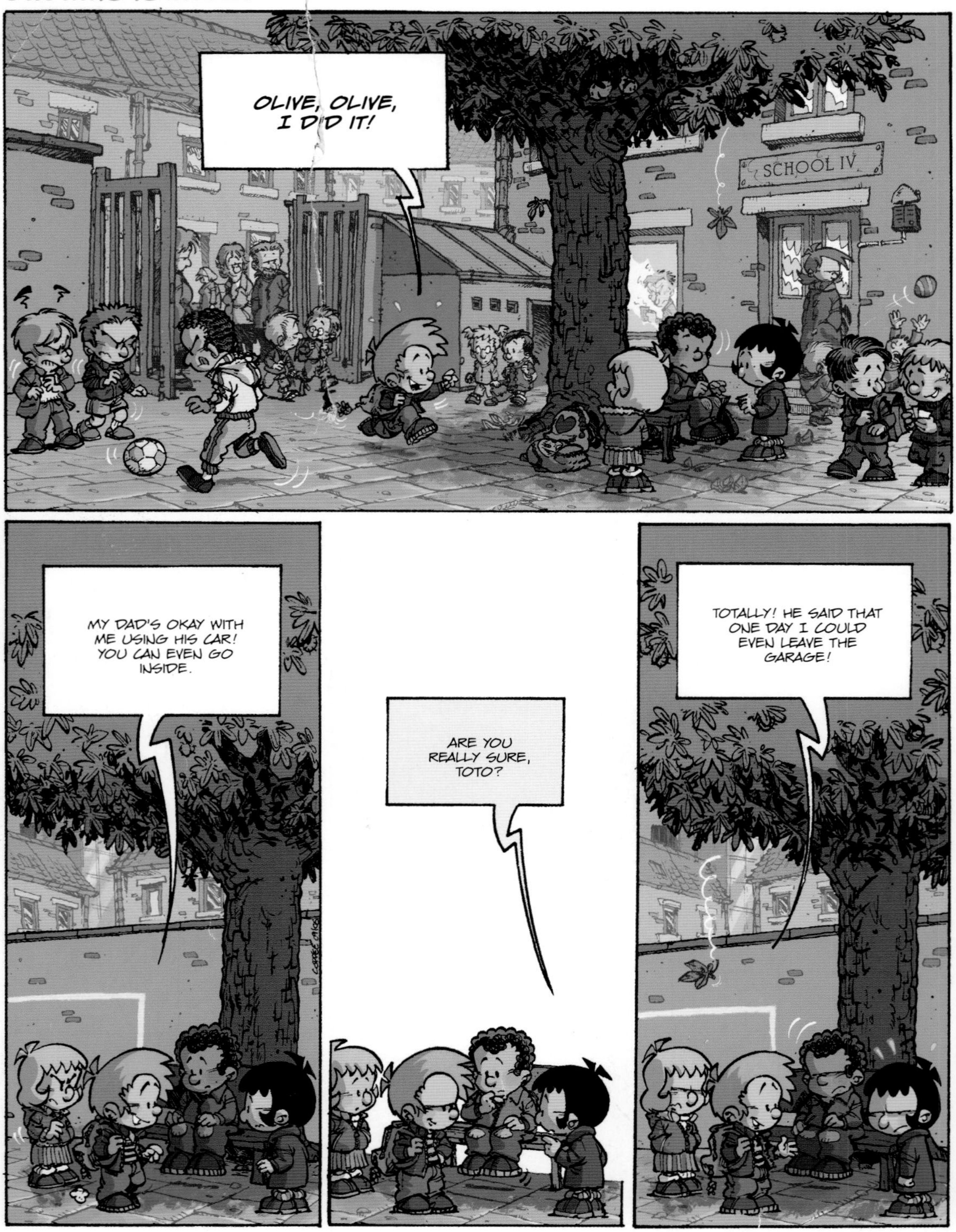
OLIVE, OLIVE, I DID IT!
SCHOOL IV
MY DAD'S OKAY WITH ME USING HIS CAR! YOU CAN EVEN GO INSIDE.
ARE YOU REALLY SURE, TOTO?
TOTALLY! HE SAID THAT ONE DAY I COULD EVEN LEAVE THE GARAGE!

Taste and Colors

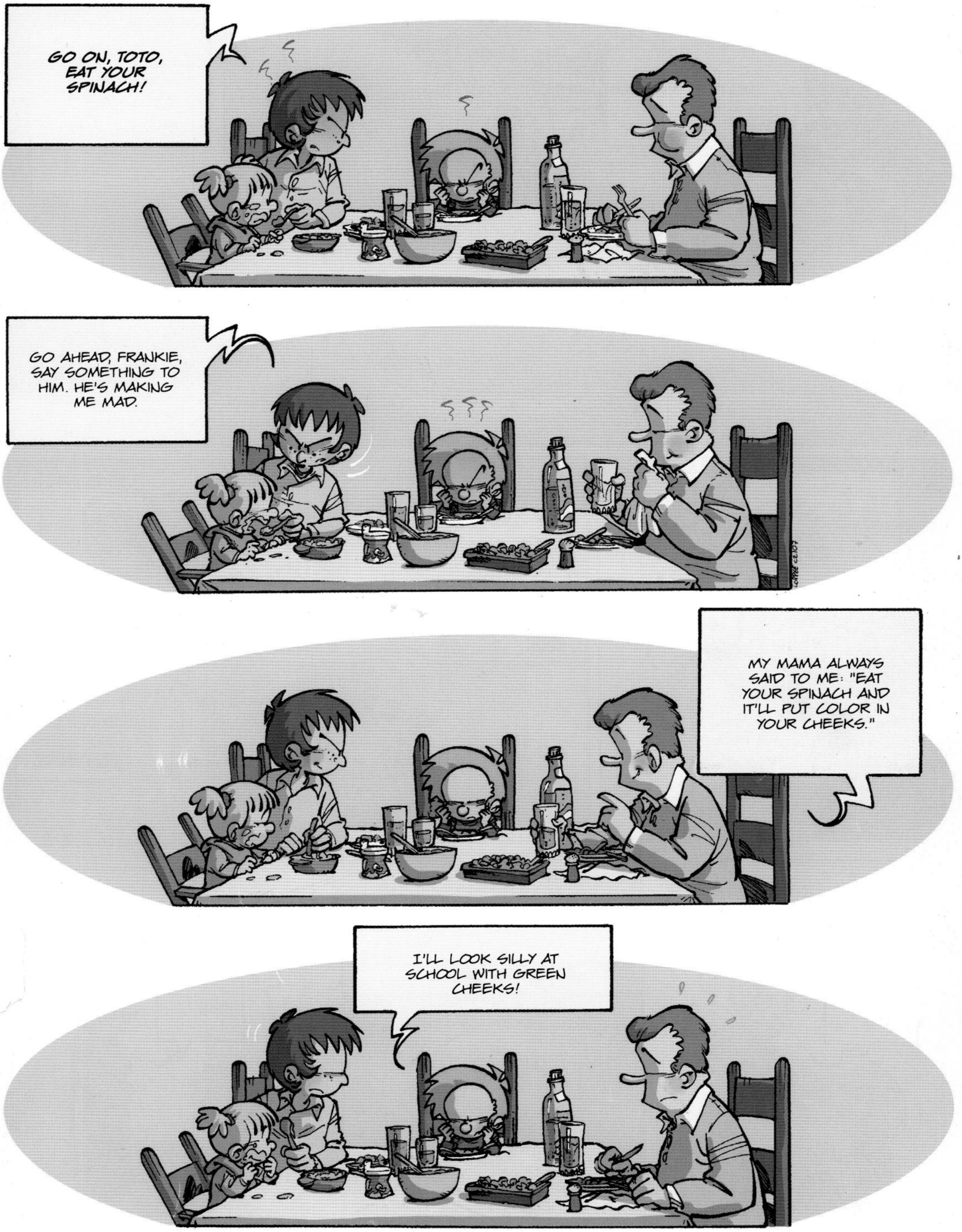
GO ON, TOTO, EAT YOUR SPINACH!
GO AHEAD, FRANKIE, SAY SOMETHING TO HIM. HE'S MAKING ME MAD.
MY MAMA ALWAYS SAID TO ME: "EAT YOUR SPINACH AND IT'LL PUT COLOR IN YOUR CHEEKS."
I'LL LOOK SILLY AT SCHOOL WITH GREEN CHEEKS!

If He's Thirsty...

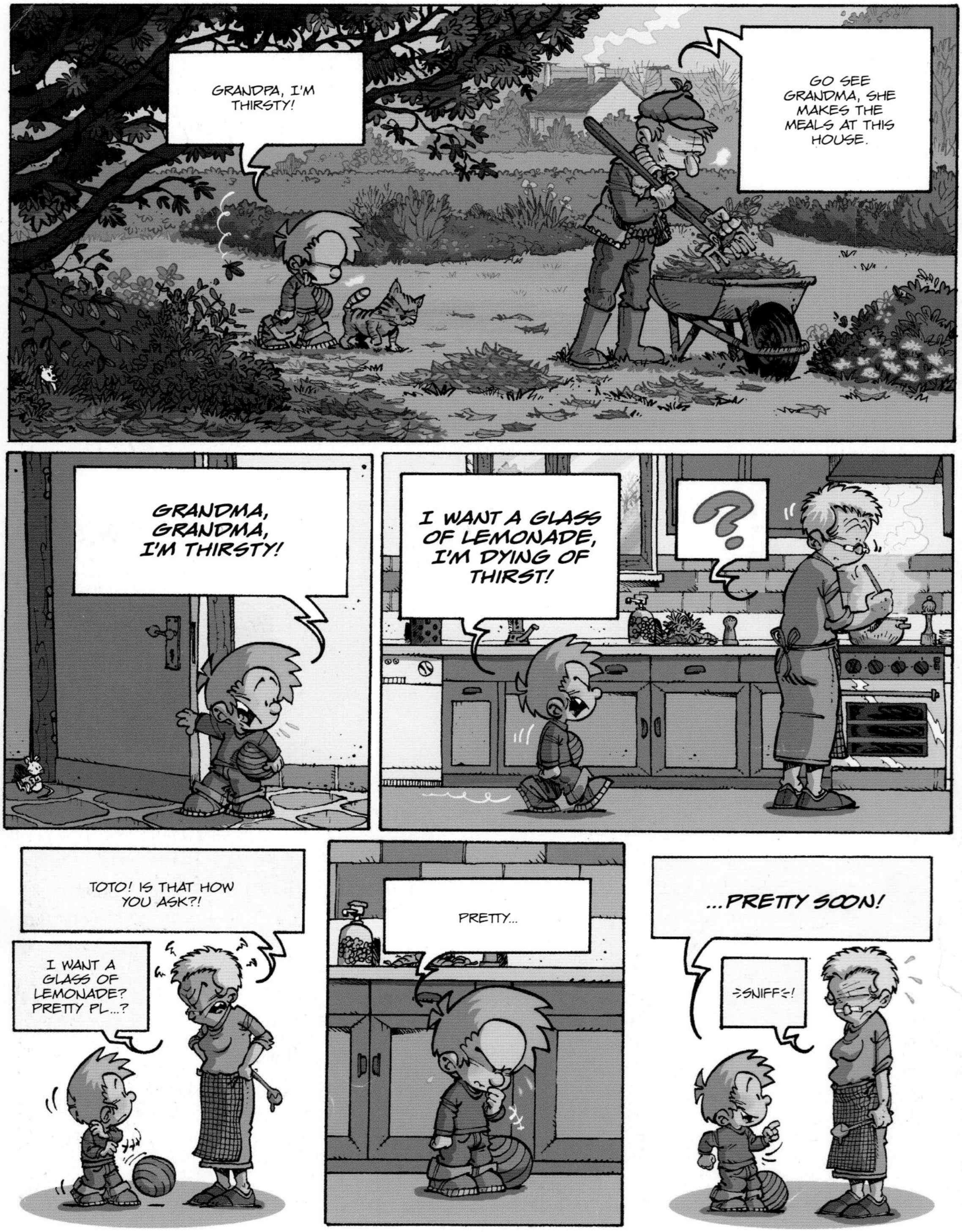

GRANDPA, I'M THIRSTY!
GO SEE GRANDMA, SHE MAKES THE MEALS AT THIS HOUSE.
GRANDMA, GRANDMA, I'M THIRSTY!
I WANT A GLASS OF LEMONADE, I'M DYING OF THIRST!
?
TOTO! IS THAT HOW YOU ASK?!
I WANT A GLASS OF LEMONADE? PRETTY PL...?
PRETTY...
...PRETTY SOON!
SNIFF!

Leaf and Fruit

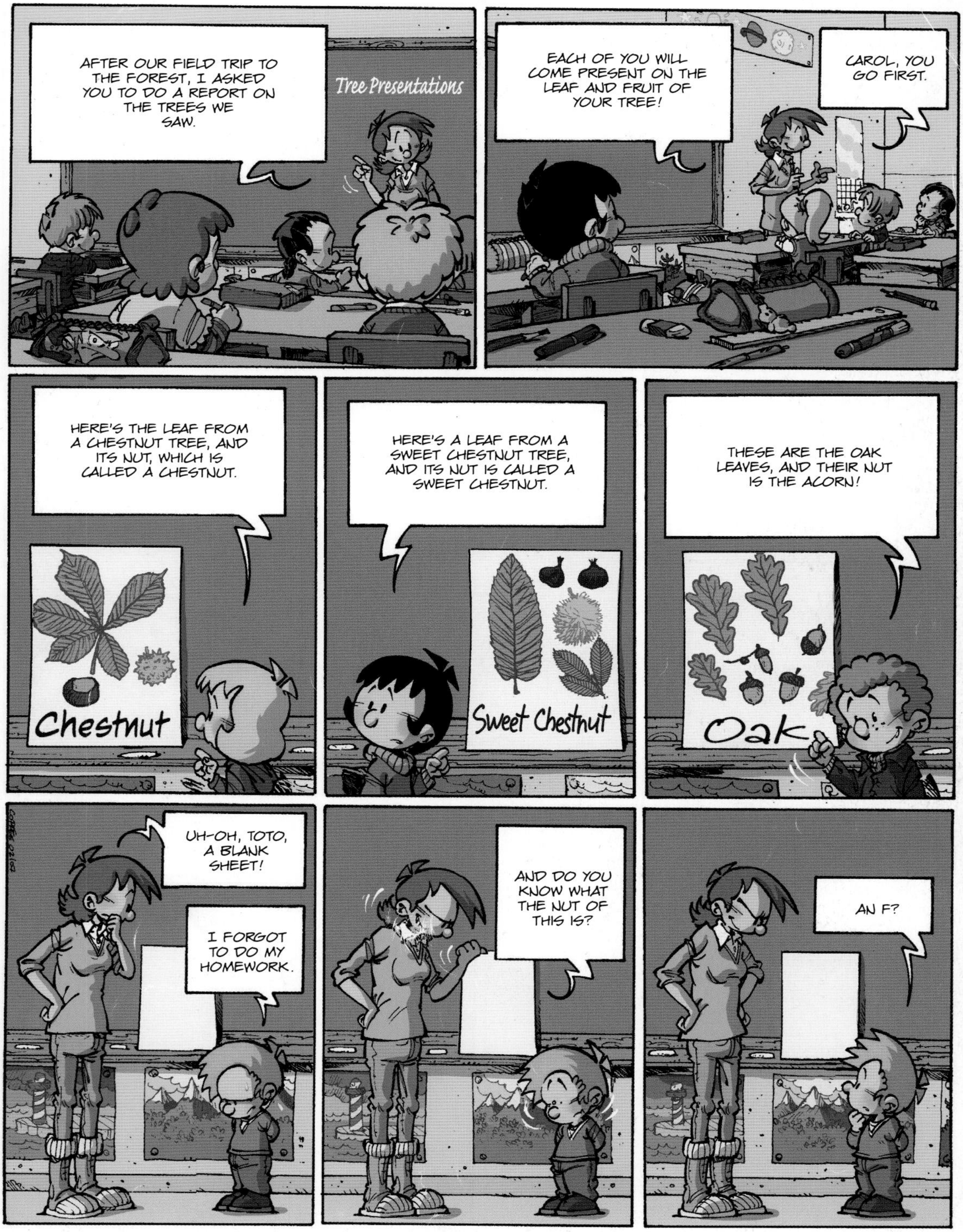
AFTER OUR FIELD TRIP TO THE FOREST, I ASKED YOU TO DO A REPORT ON THE TREES WE SAW.
Tree Presentations
EACH OF YOU WILL COME PRESENT ON THE LEAF AND FRUIT OF YOUR TREE!
CAROL, YOU GO FIRST.
HERE'S THE LEAF FROM A CHESTNUT TREE, AND ITS NUT, WHICH IS CALLED A CHESTNUT.
Chestnut
HERE'S A LEAF FROM A SWEET CHESTNUT TREE, AND ITS NUT IS CALLED A SWEET CHESTNUT.
Sweet Chestnut
THESE ARE THE OAK LEAVES, AND THEIR NUT IS THE ACORN!
Oak
UH-OH, TOTO, A BLANK SHEET!
I FORGOT TO DO MY HOMEWORK.
AND DO YOU KNOW WHAT THE NUT OF THIS IS?
AN F?

Same-erized

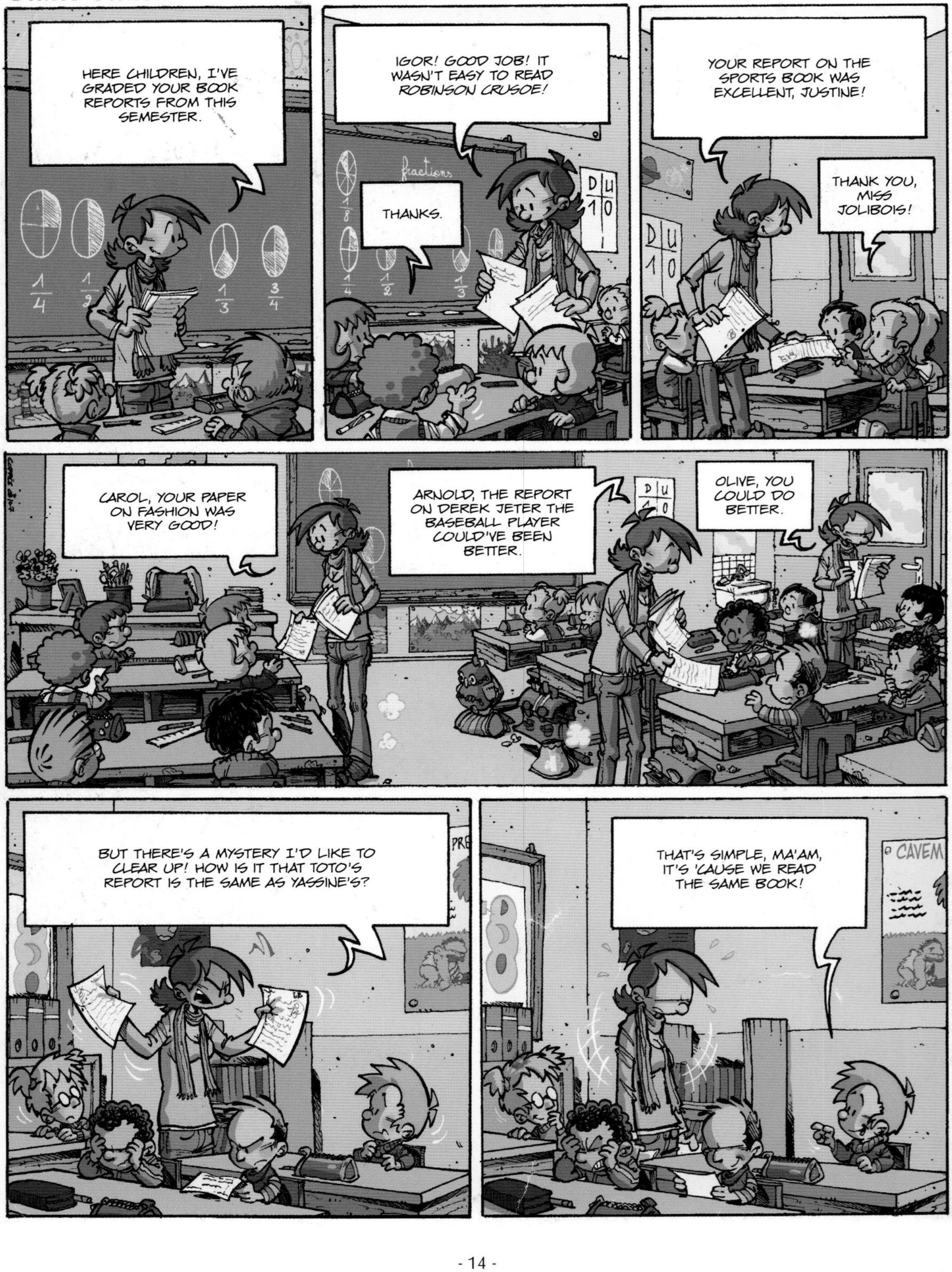
HERE CHILDREN, I'VE GRADED YOUR BOOK REPORTS FROM THIS SEMESTER.
IGOR! GOOD JOB! IT WASN'T EASY TO READ ROBINSON CRUSOE!
THANKS.
YOUR REPORT ON THE SPORTS BOOK WAS EXCELLENT, JUSTINE!
THANK YOU, MISS JOLIBOIS!
CAROL, YOUR PAPER ON FASHION WAS VERY GOOD!
ARNOLD, THE REPORT ON DEREK JETER THE BASEBALL PLAYER COULD'VE BEEN BETTER.
OLIVE, YOU COULD DO BETTER.
BUT THERE'S A MYSTERY I'D LIKE TO CLEAR UP! HOW IS IT THAT TOTO'S REPORT IS THE SAME AS YASSINE'S?
THAT'S SIMPLE, MA'AM, IT'S 'CAUSE WE READ THE SAME BOOK!

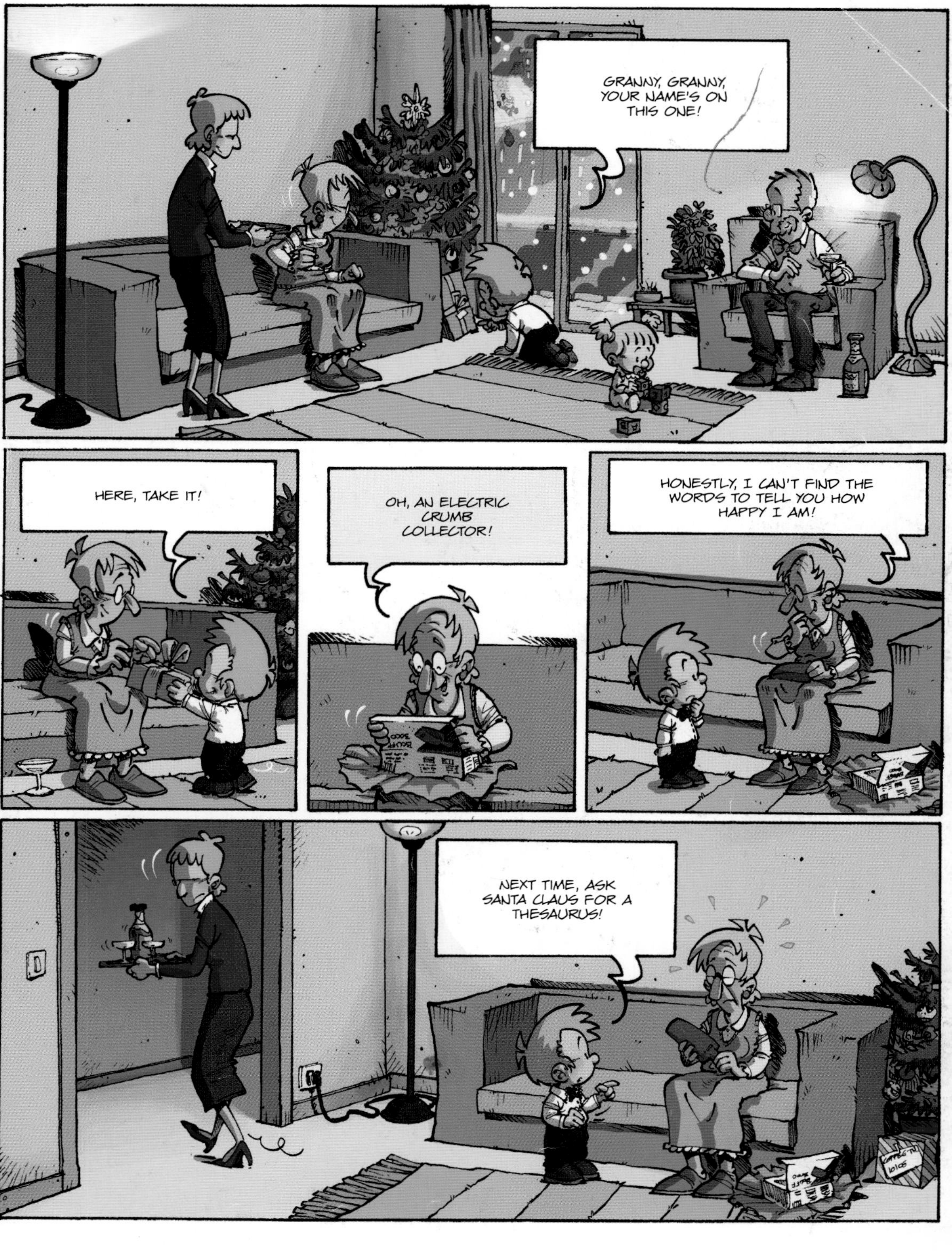
GRANNY, GRANNY, YOUR NAME'S ON THIS ONE!
HERE, TAKE IT!
OH, AN ELECTRIC CRUMB COLLECTOR!
HONESTLY, I CAN'T FIND THE WORDS TO TELL YOU HOW HAPPY I AM!
NEXT TIME, ASK SANTA CLAUS FOR A THESAURUS!

Mimicry's Limits

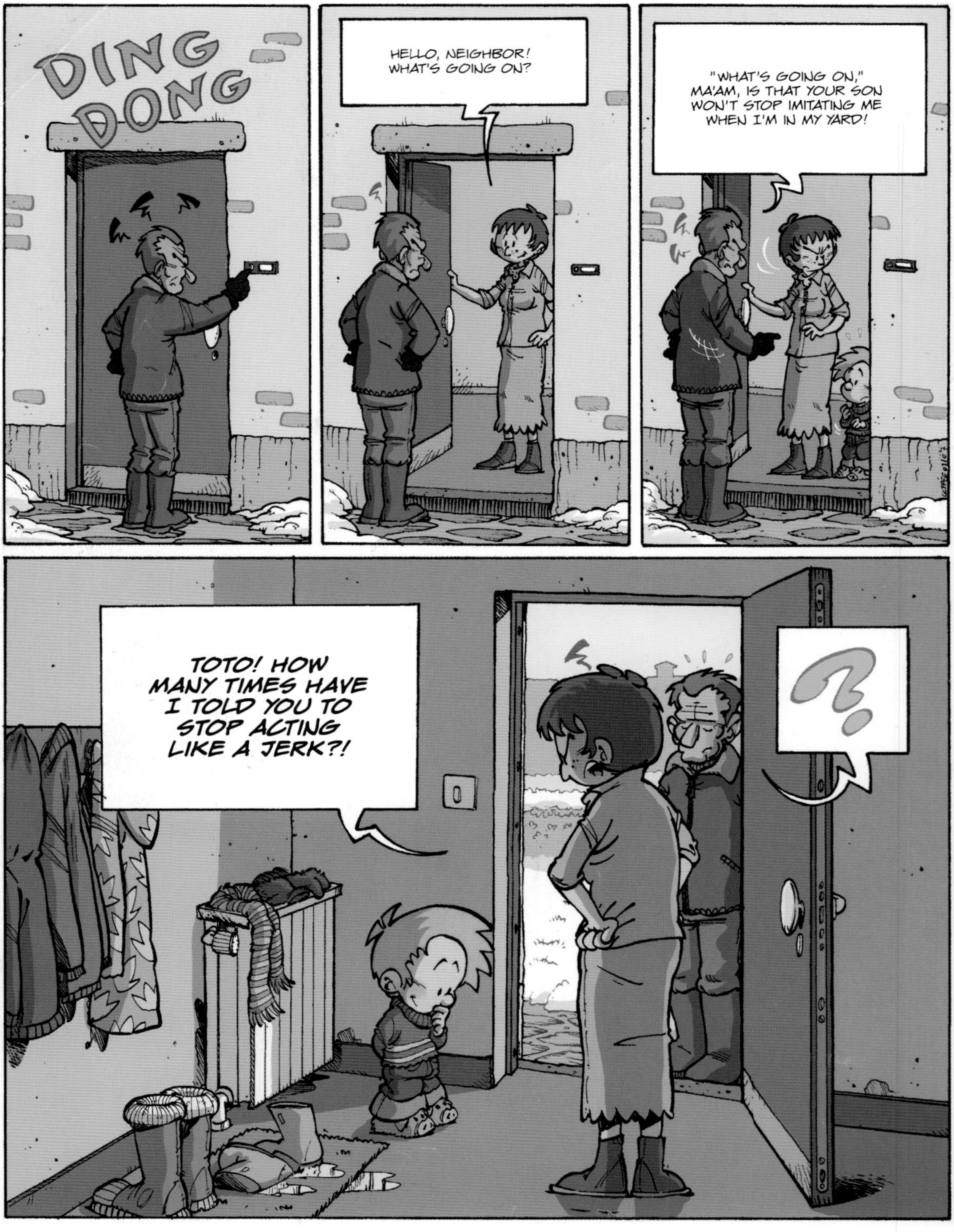
DING DONG
HELLO, NEIGHBOR! WHAT'S GOING ON?
"WHAT'S GOING ON," MA'AM, IS THAT YOUR SON WON'T STOP IMITATING ME WHEN I'M IN MY YARD!
TOTO! HOW MANY TIMES HAVE I TOLD YOU TO STOP ACTING LIKE A JERK?!
?

I Lost My Hanky

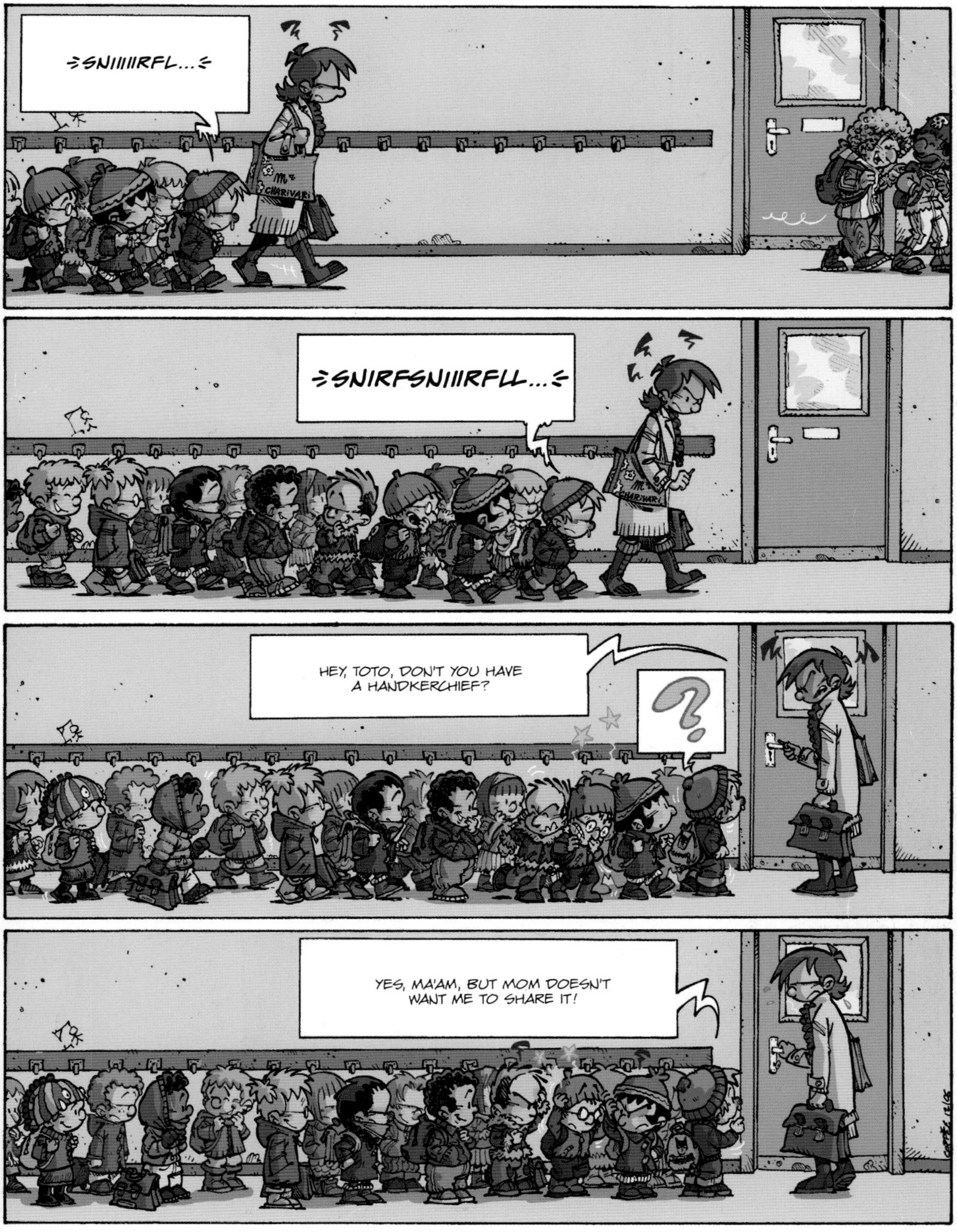

=SNIIIIRFL...=
=SNIRFSNIIIRFLL...=
HEY, TOTO, DON'T YOU HAVE A HANDKERCHIEF?
?
YES, MA'AM, BUT MOM DOESN'T WANT ME TO SHARE IT!

Future Career

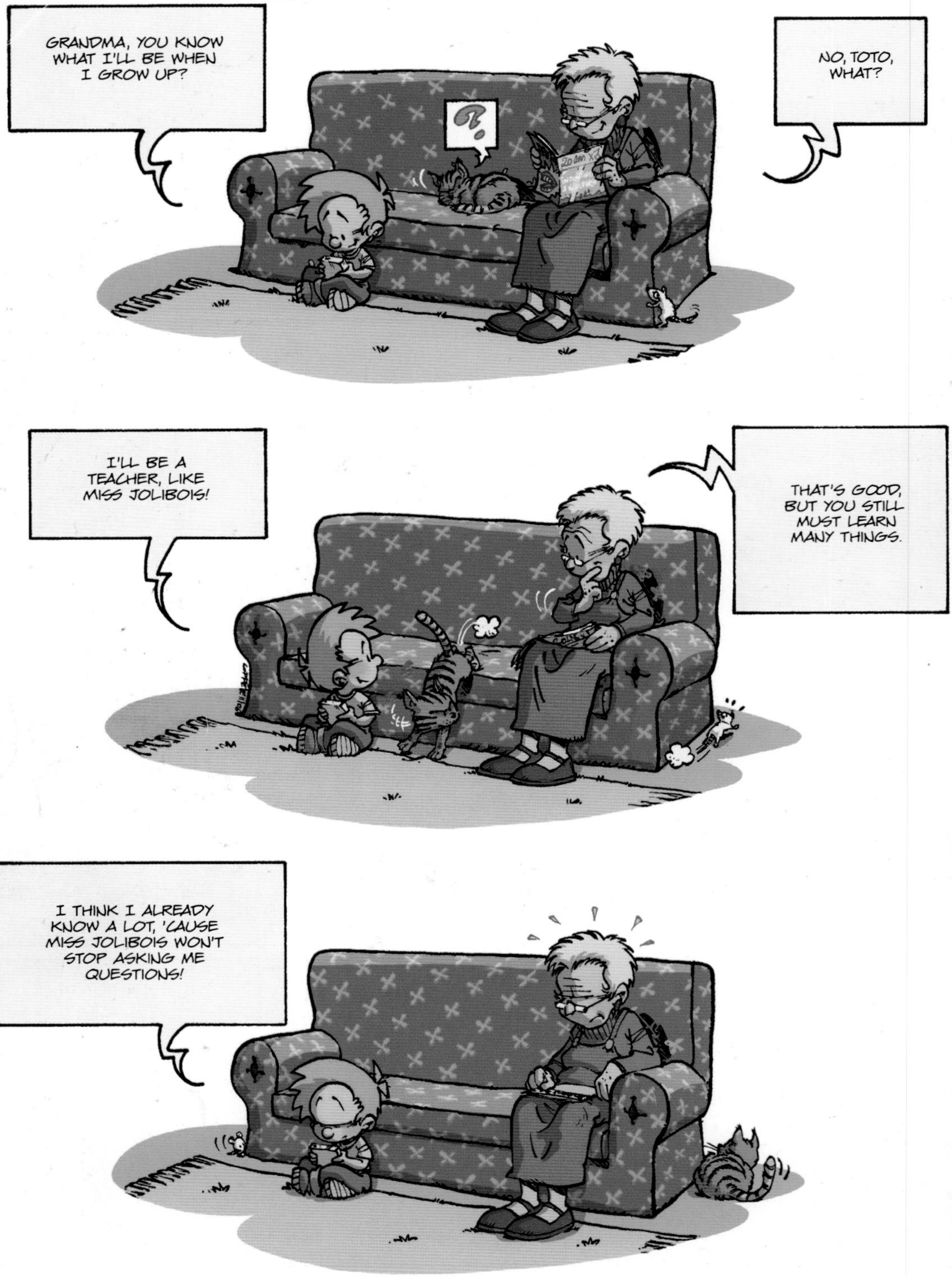
GRANDMA, YOU KNOW WHAT I'LL BE WHEN I GROW UP?
NO, TOTO, WHAT?
I'LL BE A TEACHER, LIKE MISS JOLIBOIS!
THAT'S GOOD, BUT YOU STILL MUST LEARN MANY THINGS.
I THINK I ALREADY KNOW A LOT, 'CAUSE MISS JOLIBOIS WON'T STOP ASKING ME QUESTIONS!

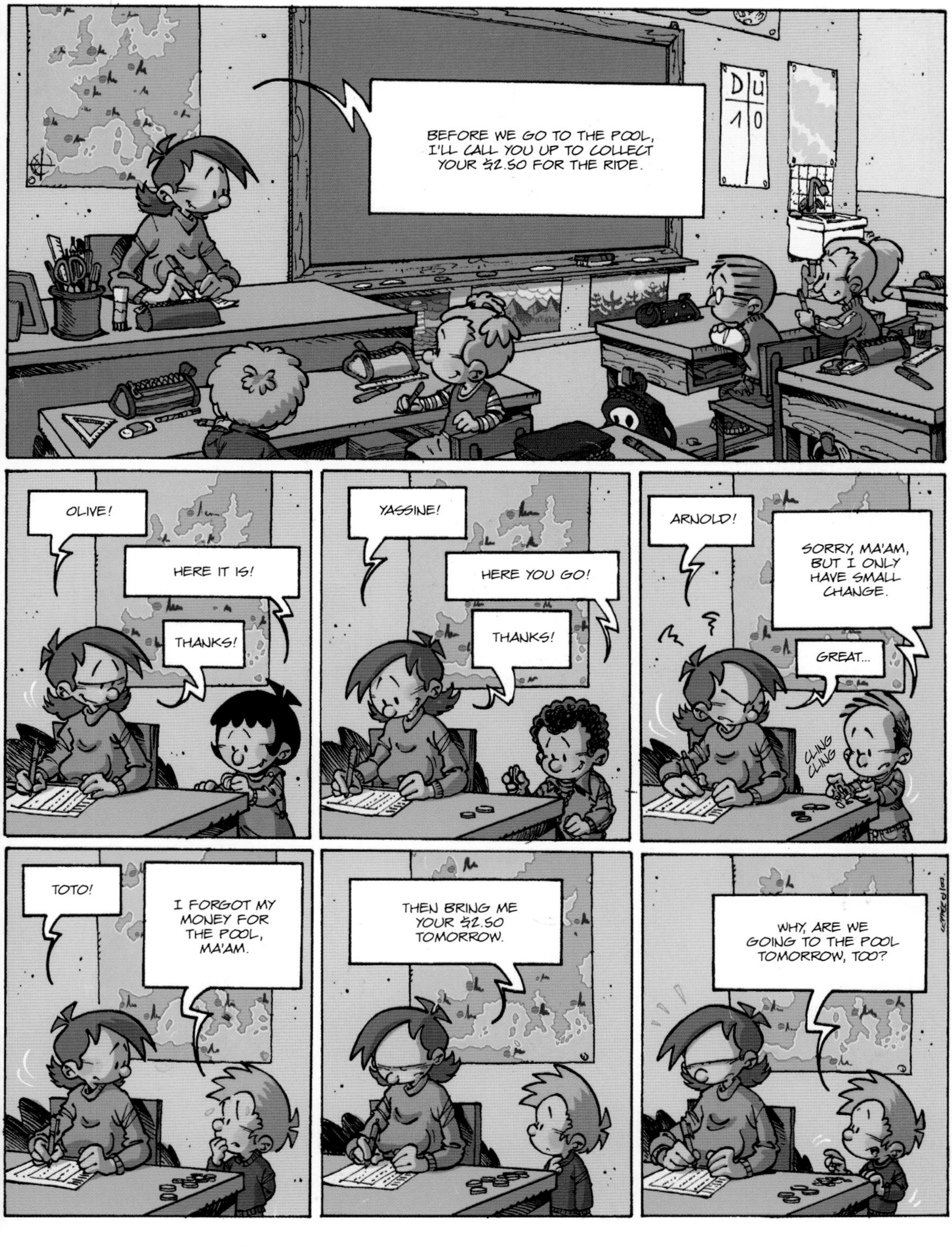
BEFORE WE GO TO THE POOL, I'LL CALL YOU UP TO COLLECT YOUR $2.50 FOR THE RIDE.
OLIVE!
HERE IT IS!
THANKS!
YASSINE!
HERE YOU GO!
THANKS!
ARNOLD!
SORRY, MA'AM, BUT I ONLY HAVE SMALL CHANGE.
GREAT...
CLING CLING
TOTO!
I FORGOT MY MONEY FOR THE POOL, MA'AM.
THEN BRING ME YOUR $2.50 TOMORROW.
WHY, ARE WE GOING TO THE POOL TOMORROW, TOO?

Cleaning Up a Mess

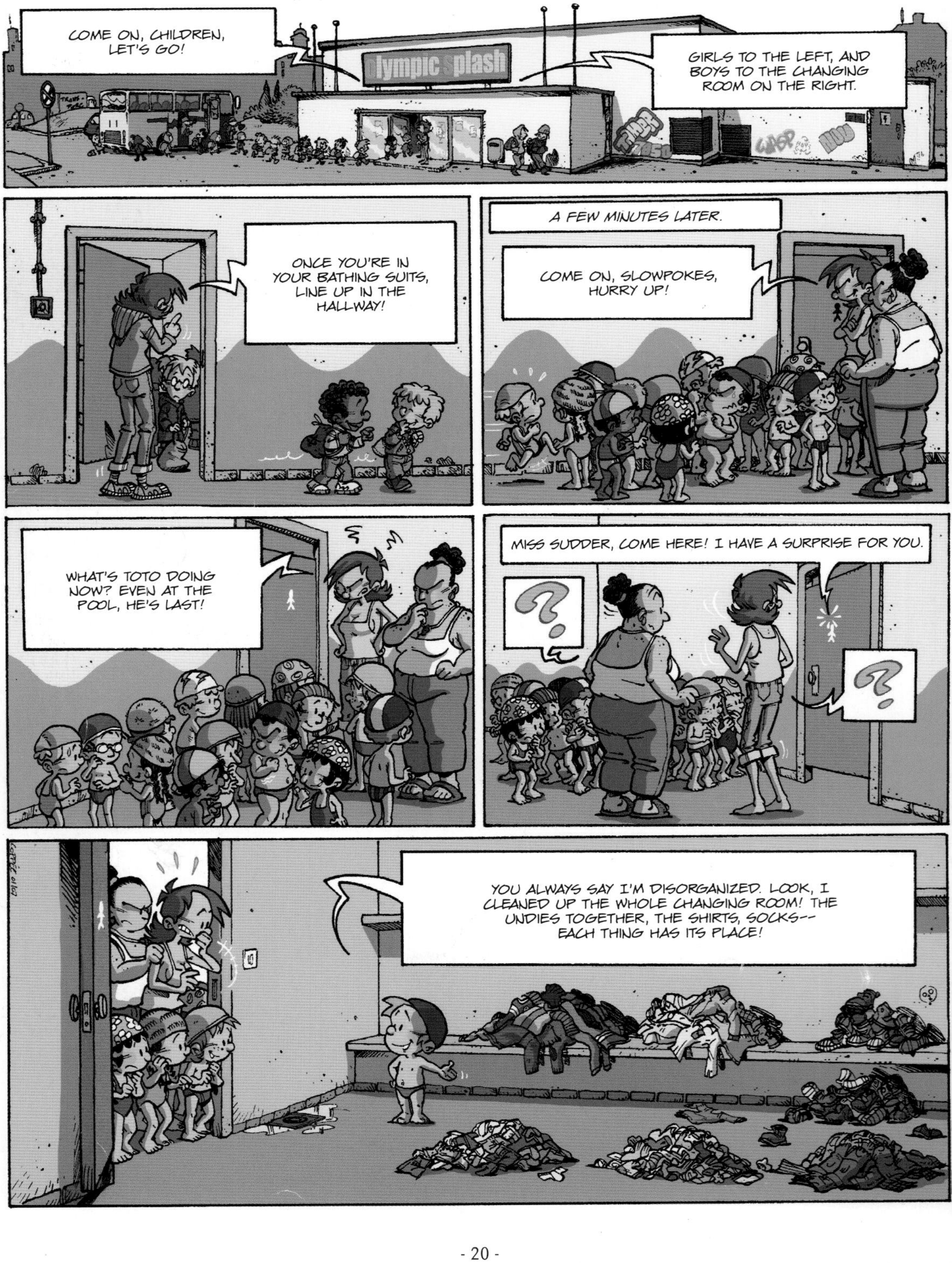

COME ON, CHILDREN, LET'S GO!
olympic Splash
GIRLS TO THE LEFT, AND BOYS TO THE CHANGING ROOM ON THE RIGHT.
ONCE YOU'RE IN YOUR BATHING SUITS, LINE UP IN THE HALLWAY!
A FEW MINUTES LATER.
COME ON, SLOWPOKES, HURRY UP!
WHAT'S TOTO DOING NOW? EVEN AT THE POOL, HE'S LAST!
MISS SUDDER, COME HERE! I HAVE A SURPRISE FOR YOU.
?
?
YOU ALWAYS SAY I'M DISORGANIZED. LOOK, I CLEANED UP THE WHOLE CHANGING ROOM! THE UNDIES TOGETHER, THE SHIRTS, SOCKS-- EACH THING HAS ITS PLACE!

Water Courses

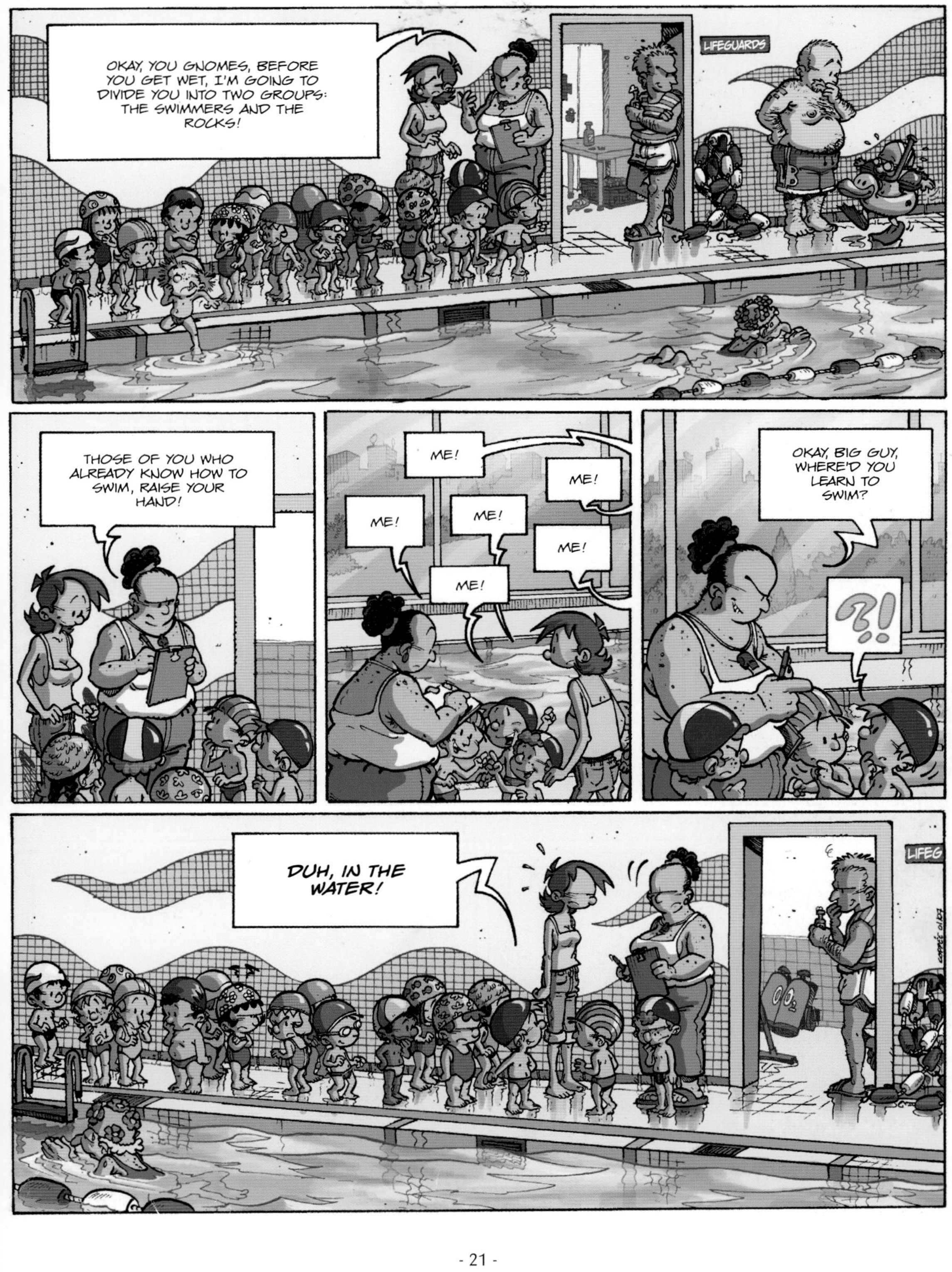

OKAY, YOU GNOMES, BEFORE YOU GET WET, I'M GOING TO DIVIDE YOU INTO TWO GROUPS: THE SWIMMERS AND THE ROCKS!
LIFEGUARDS
THOSE OF YOU WHO ALREADY KNOW HOW TO SWIM, RAISE YOUR HAND!
ME!
ME!
ME!
ME!
ME!
ME!
OKAY, BIG GUY, WHERE'D YOU LEARN TO SWIM?
?!
DUH, IN THE WATER!
LIFEG

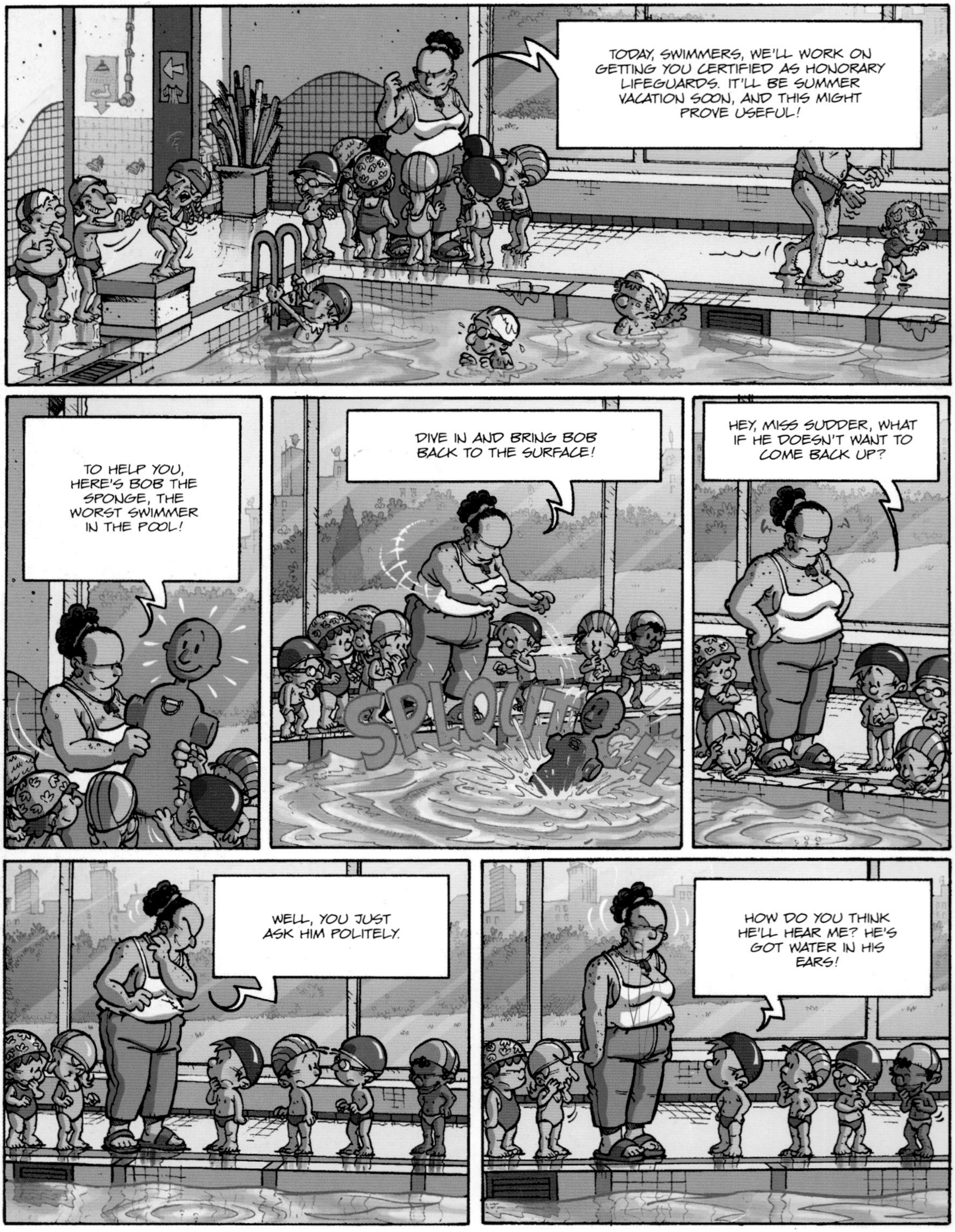
TODAY, SWIMMERS, WE'LL WORK ON GETTING YOU CERTIFIED AS HONORARY LIFEGUARDS. IT'LL BE SUMMER VACATION SOON, AND THIS MIGHT PROVE USEFUL!
TO HELP YOU, HERE'S BOB THE SPONGE, THE WORST SWIMMER IN THE POOL!
DIVE IN AND BRING BOB BACK TO THE SURFACE!
SPLOUTCH
HEY, MISS SUDDER, WHAT IF HE DOESN'T WANT TO COME BACK UP?
WELL, YOU JUST ASK HIM POLITELY.
HOW DO YOU THINK HE'LL HEAR ME? HE'S GOT WATER IN HIS EARS!

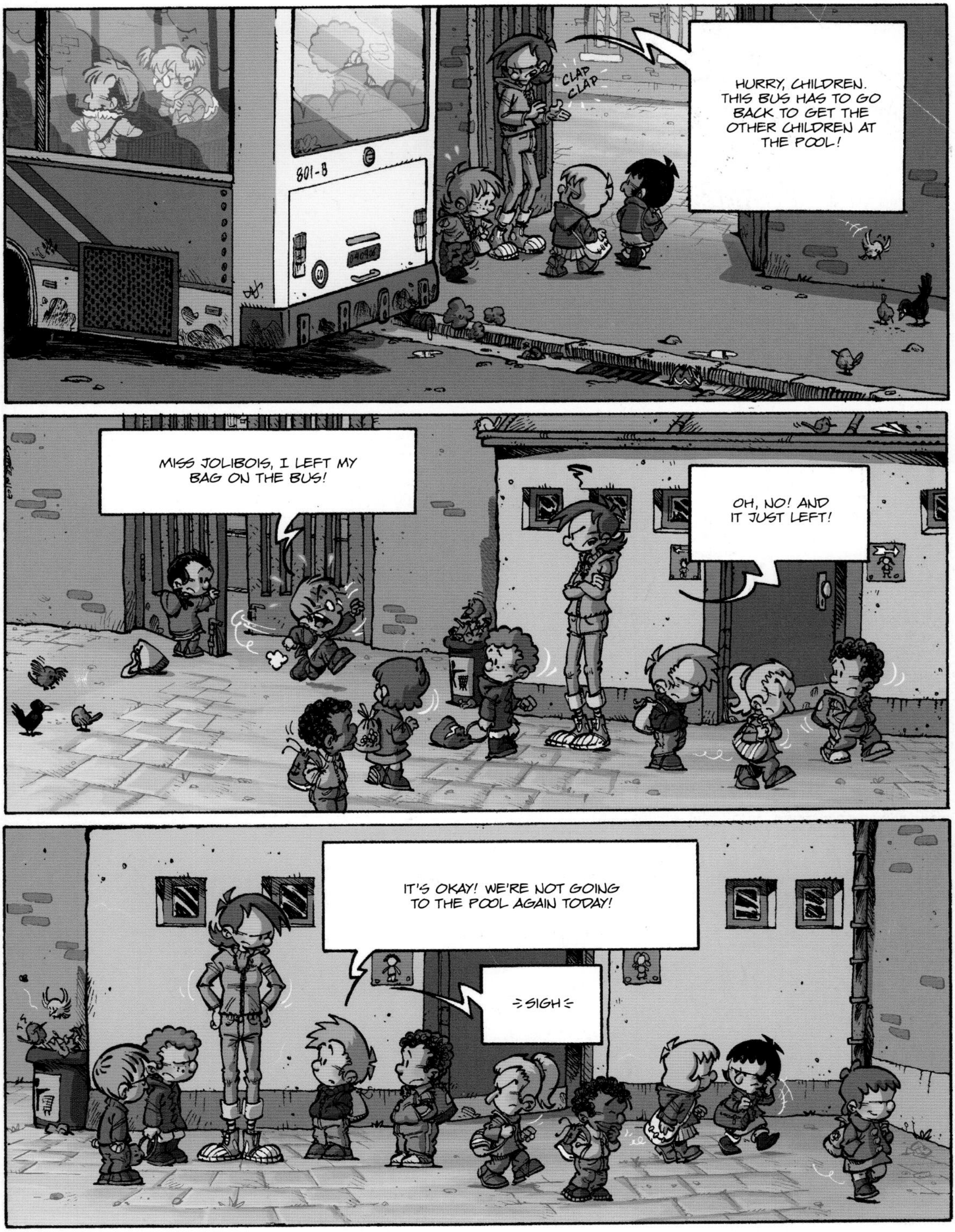
CLAP
CLAP
HURRY, CHILDREN. THIS BUS HAS TO GO BACK TO GET THE OTHER CHILDREN AT THE POOL!
801-B
MISS JOLIBOIS, I LEFT MY BAG ON THE BUS!
OH, NO! AND IT JUST LEFT!
IT'S OKAY! WE'RE NOT GOING TO THE POOL AGAIN TODAY!
SIGH

Apparently for Rent

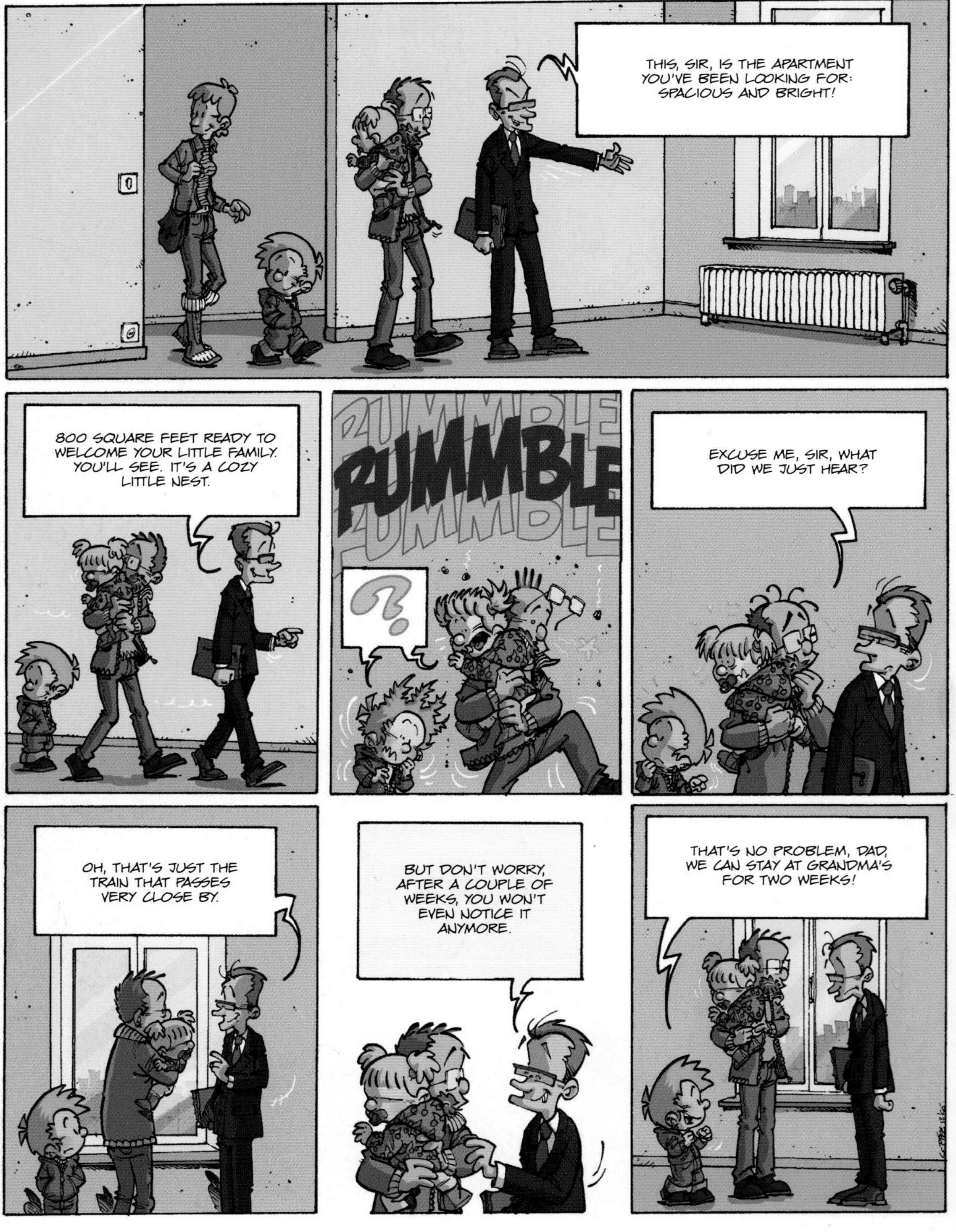
THIS, SIR, IS THE APARTMENT YOU'VE BEEN LOOKING FOR: SPACIOUS AND BRIGHT!
800 SQUARE FEET READY TO WELCOME YOUR LITTLE FAMILY. YOU'LL SEE. IT'S A COZY LITTLE NEST.
RUMMBLE
?
EXCUSE ME, SIR, WHAT DID WE JUST HEAR?
OH, THAT'S JUST THE TRAIN THAT PASSES VERY CLOSE BY.
BUT DON'T WORRY, AFTER A COUPLE OF WEEKS, YOU WON'T EVEN NOTICE IT ANYMORE.
THAT'S NO PROBLEM, DAD, WE CAN STAY AT GRANDMA'S FOR TWO WEEKS!

Give it up, Slowpoke!

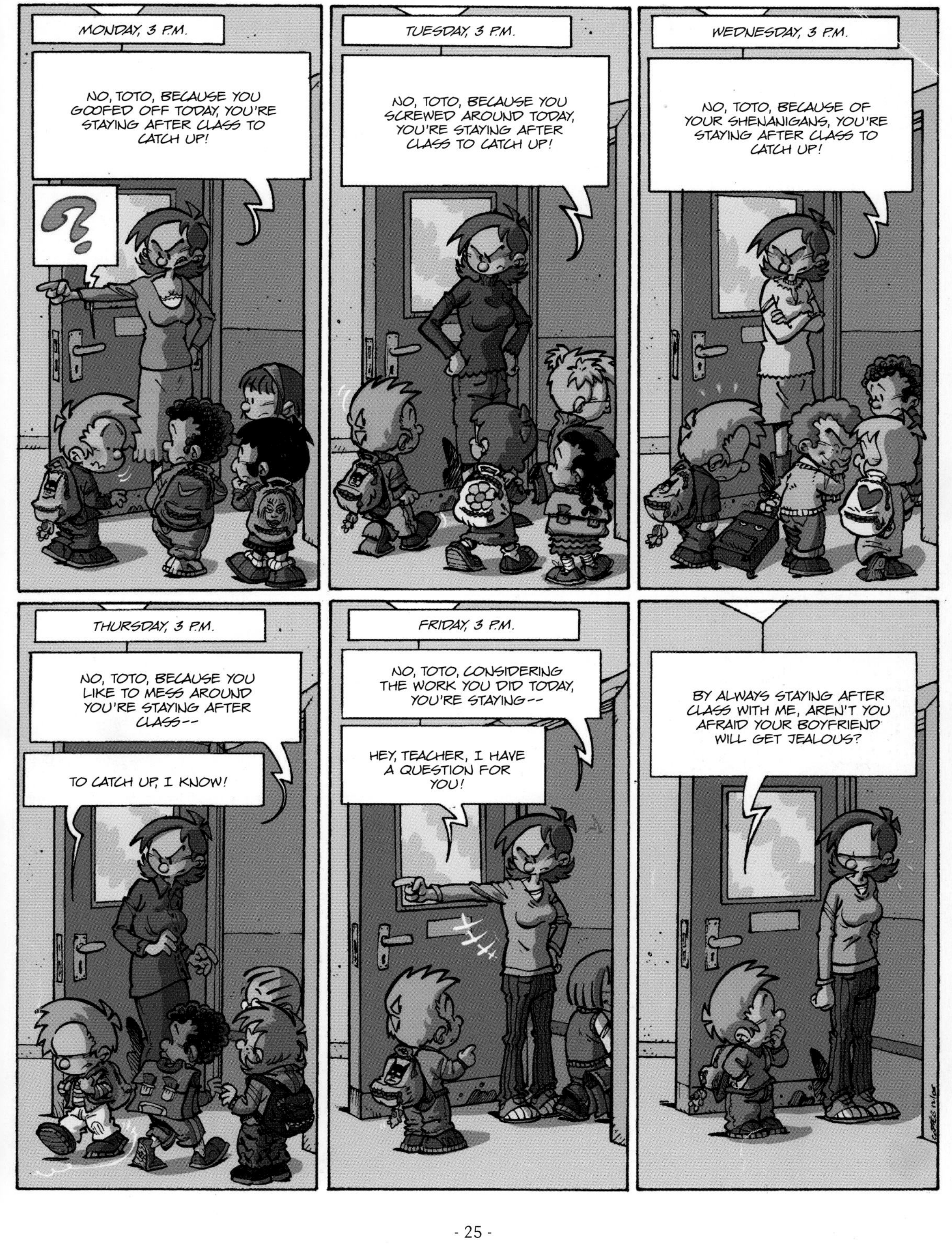
MONDAY, 3 P.M.
NO, TOTO, BECAUSE YOU GOOFED OFF TODAY, YOU'RE STAYING AFTER CLASS TO CATCH UP!
?
TUESDAY, 3 P.M.
NO, TOTO, BECAUSE YOU SCREWED AROUND TODAY, YOU'RE STAYING AFTER CLASS TO CATCH UP!
WEDNESDAY, 3 P.M.
NO, TOTO, BECAUSE OF YOUR SHENANIGANS, YOU'RE STAYING AFTER CLASS TO CATCH UP!
THURSDAY, 3 P.M.
NO, TOTO, BECAUSE YOU LIKE TO MESS AROUND YOU'RE STAYING AFTER CLASS--
TO CATCH UP, I KNOW!
FRIDAY, 3 P.M.
NO, TOTO, CONSIDERING THE WORK YOU DID TODAY, YOU'RE STAYING--
HEY, TEACHER, I HAVE A QUESTION FOR YOU!
BY ALWAYS STAYING AFTER CLASS WITH ME, AREN'T YOU AFRAID YOUR BOYFRIEND WILL GET JEALOUS?

Mockery

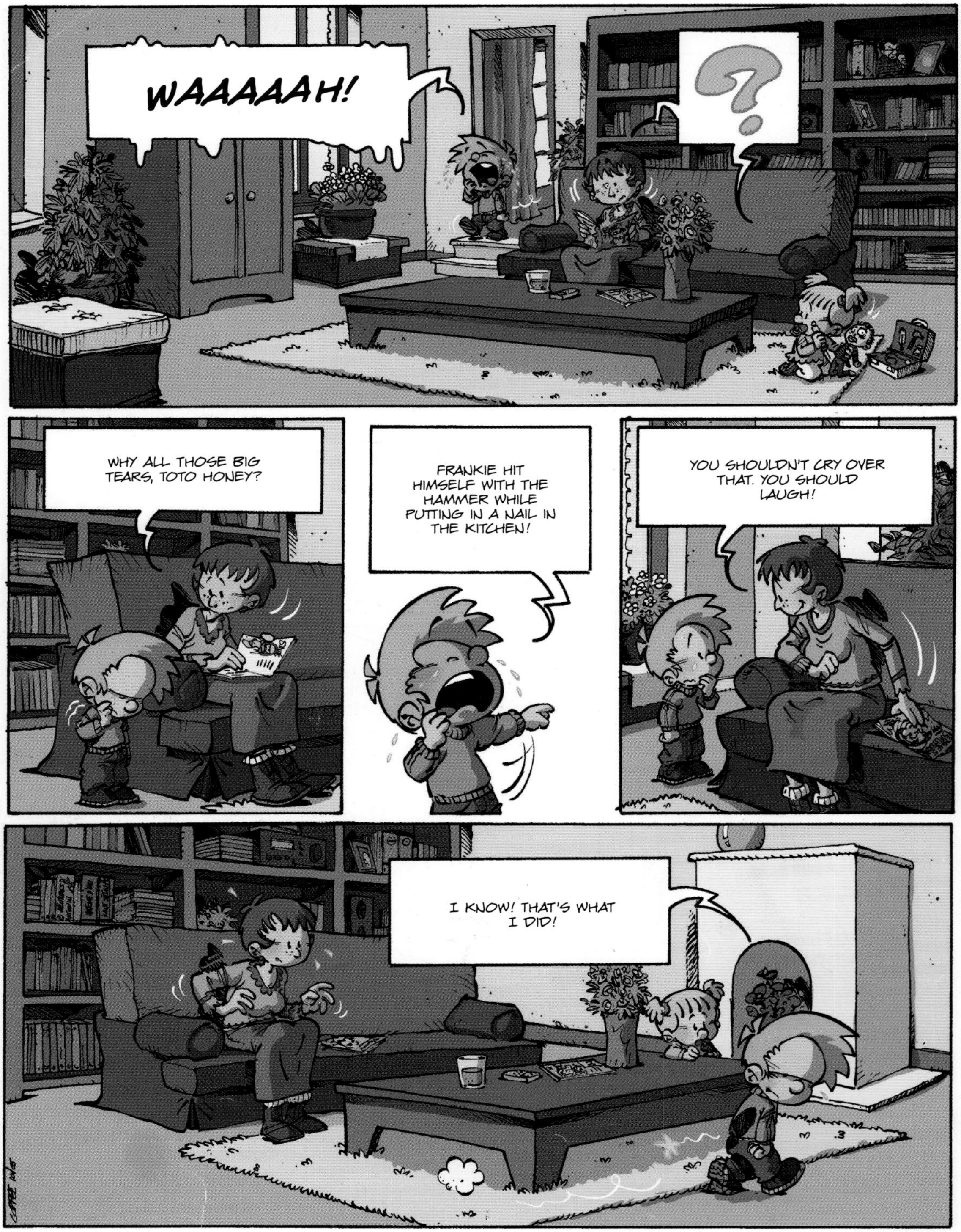
WAAAAAH!
?
WHY ALL THOSE BIG TEARS, TOTO HONEY?
FRANKIE HIT HIMSELF WITH THE HAMMER WHILE PUTTING IN A NAIL IN THE KITCHEN!
YOU SHOULDN'T CRY OVER THAT. YOU SHOULD LAUGH!
I KNOW! THAT'S WHAT I DID!

A Fool's Reminder

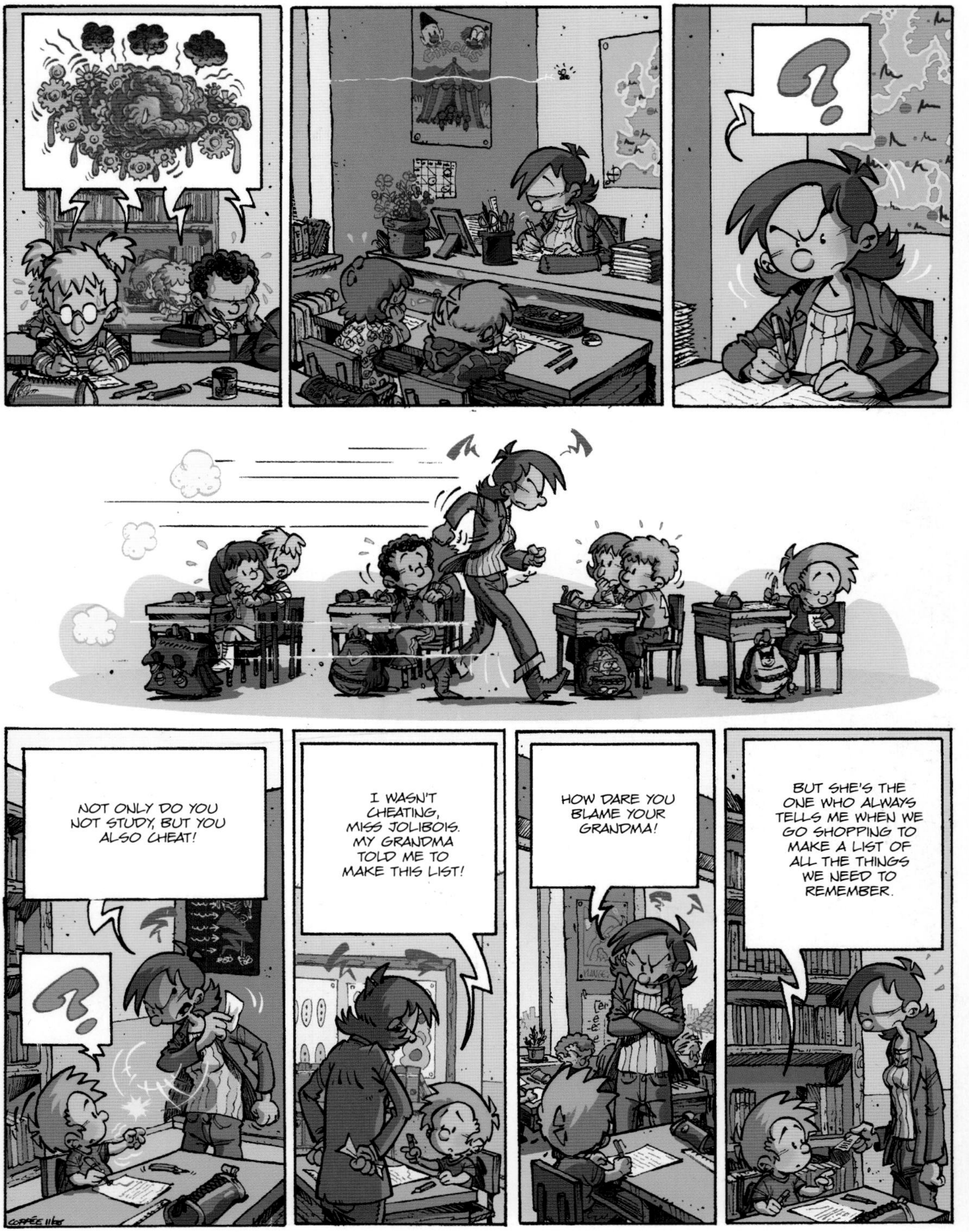
?
NOT ONLY DO YOU NOT STUDY, BUT YOU ALSO CHEAT!
?
I WASN'T CHEATING, MISS JOLIBOIS. MY GRANDMA TOLD ME TO MAKE THIS LIST!
HOW DARE YOU BLAME YOUR GRANDMA!
BUT SHE'S THE ONE WHO ALWAYS TELLS ME WHEN WE GO SHOPPING TO MAKE A LIST OF ALL THE THINGS WE NEED TO REMEMBER.

Zero Calories!

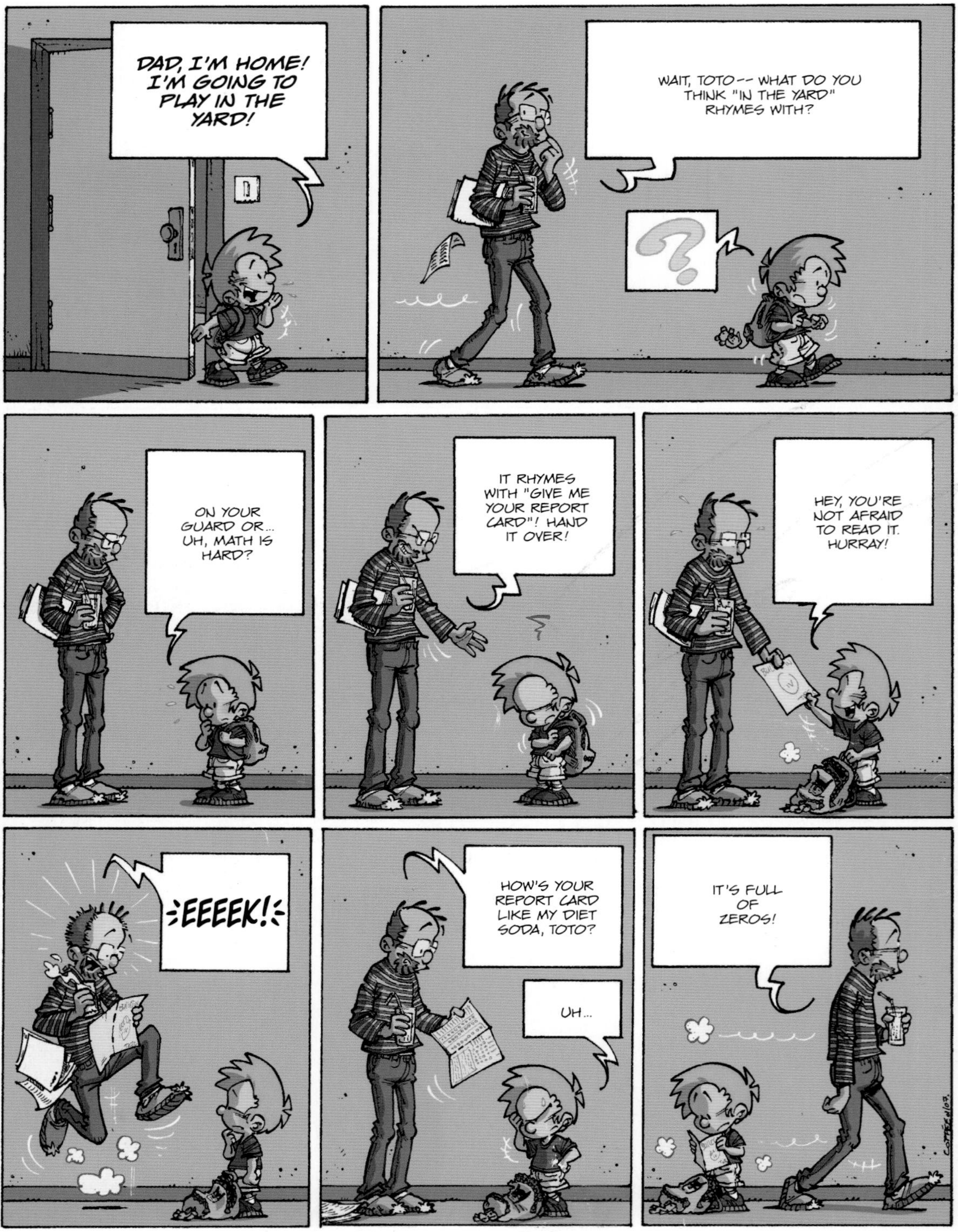
DAD, I'M HOME! I'M GOING TO PLAY IN THE YARD!
WAIT, TOTO-- WHAT DO YOU THINK "IN THE YARD" RHYMES WITH?
?
ON YOUR GUARD OR... UH, MATH IS HARD?
IT RHYMES WITH "GIVE ME YOUR REPORT CARD"! HAND IT OVER!
HEY, YOU'RE NOT AFRAID TO READ IT. HURRAY!
EEEEK!
HOW'S YOUR REPORT CARD LIKE MY DIET SODA, TOTO?
UH...
IT'S FULL OF ZEROS!

Milk Capacities

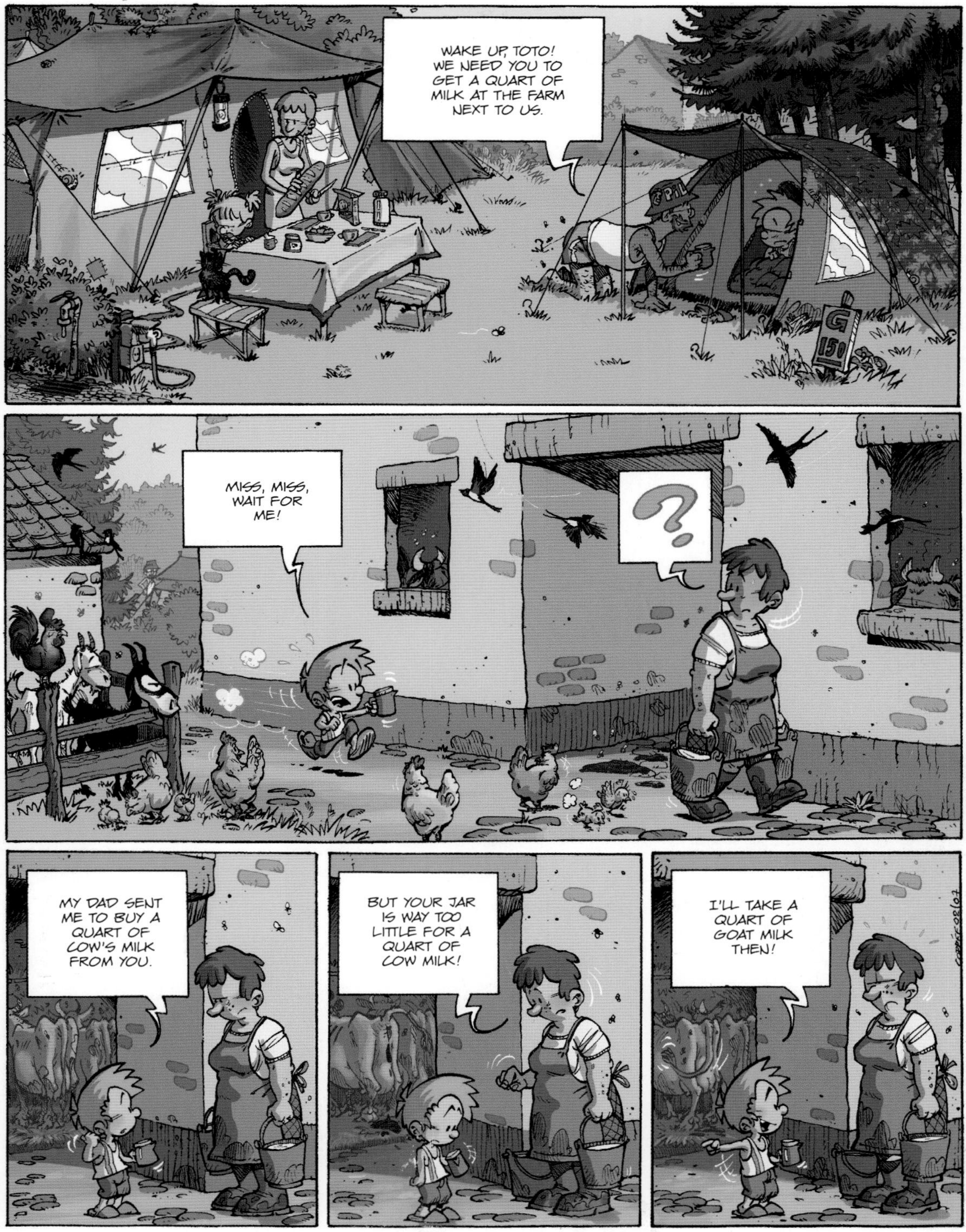
WAKE UP, TOTO! WE NEED YOU TO GET A QUART OF MILK AT THE FARM NEXT TO US.
MISS, MISS, WAIT FOR ME!
?
MY DAD SENT ME TO BUY A QUART OF COW'S MILK FROM YOU.
BUT YOUR JAR IS WAY TOO LITTLE FOR A QUART OF COW MILK!
I'LL TAKE A QUART OF GOAT MILK THEN!

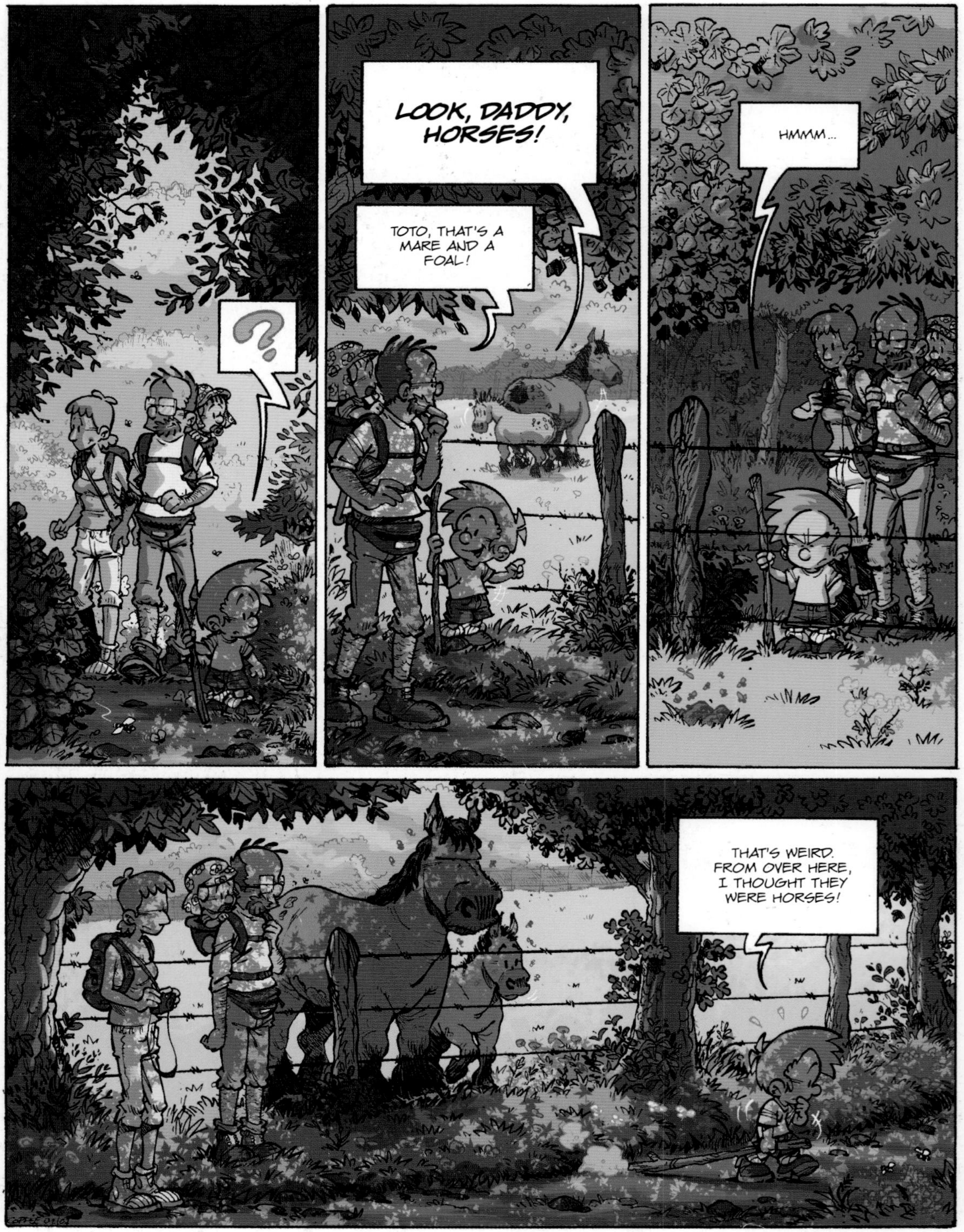
?
LOOK, DADDY, HORSES!
TOTO, THAT'S A MARE AND A FOAL!
HMMM...
THAT'S WEIRD. FROM OVER HERE, I THOUGHT THEY WERE HORSES!

The Fruits of Theft

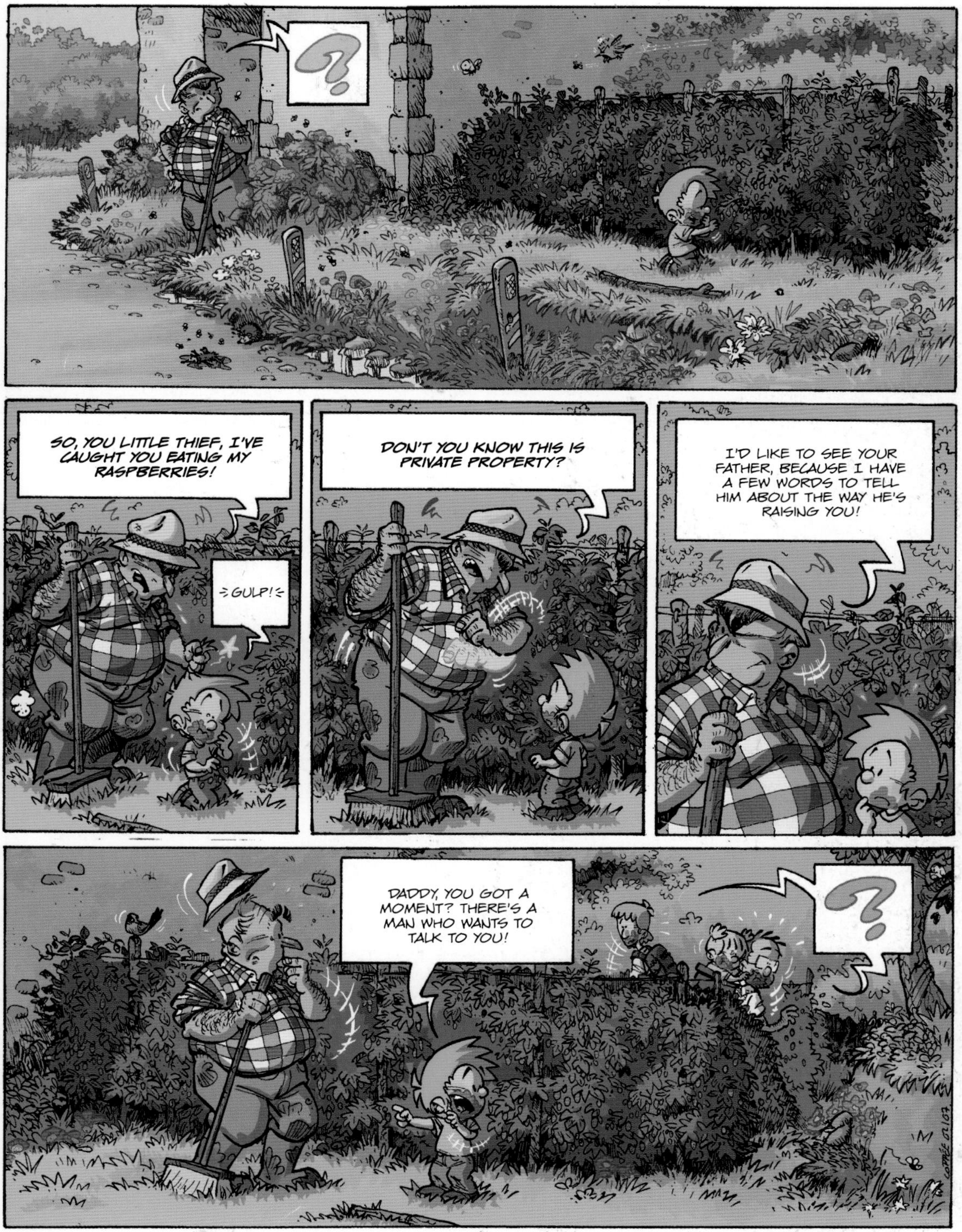
?
SO, YOU LITTLE THIEF, I'VE CAUGHT YOU EATING MY RASPBERRIES!
GULP!
DON'T YOU KNOW THIS IS PRIVATE PROPERTY?
I'D LIKE TO SEE YOUR FATHER, BECAUSE I HAVE A FEW WORDS TO TELL HIM ABOUT THE WAY HE'S RAISING YOU!
DADDY, YOU GOT A MOMENT? THERE'S A MAN WHO WANTS TO TALK TO YOU!
?

The Next Day

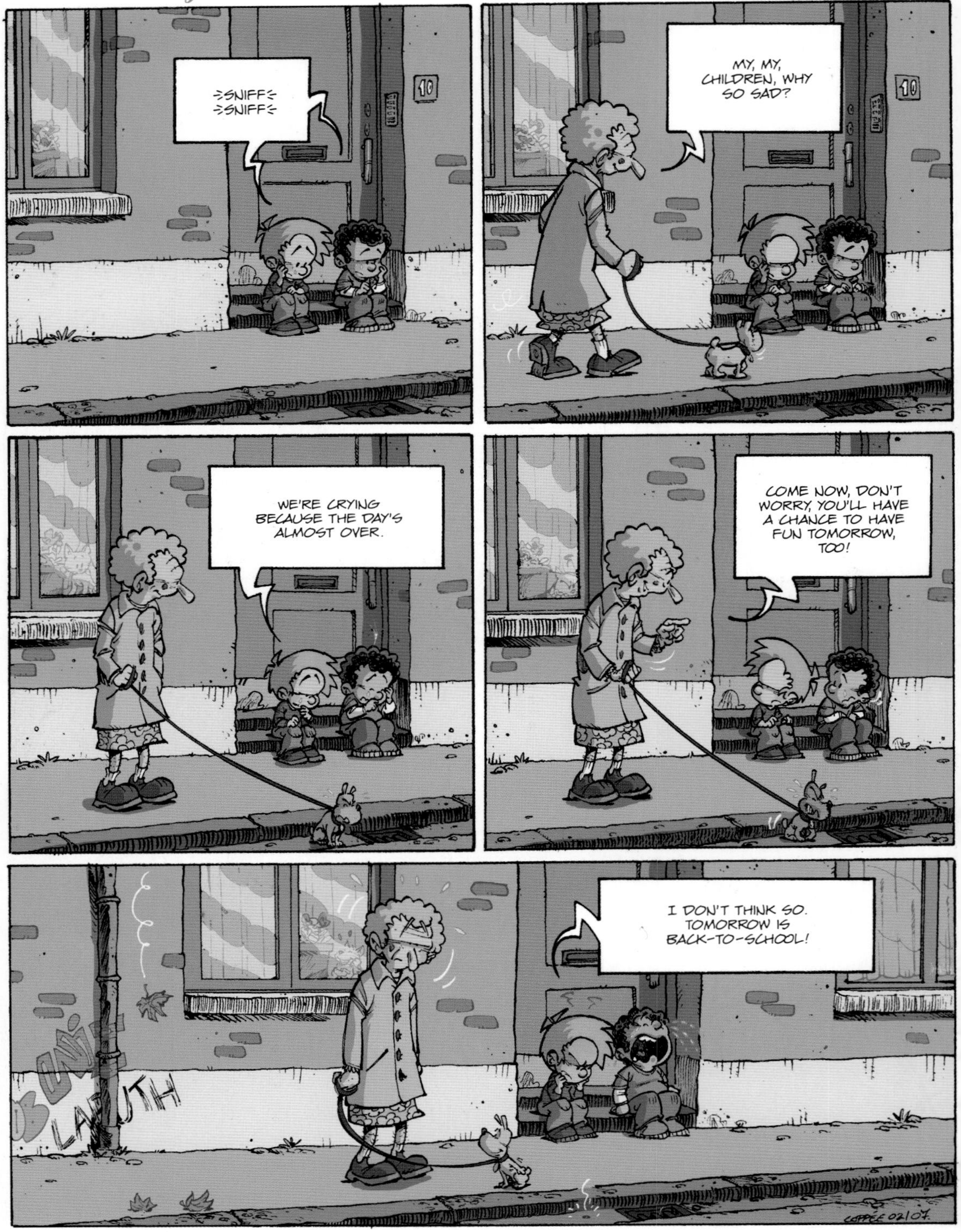

=SNIFF= =SNIFF=
MY, MY, CHILDREN, WHY SO SAD?
WE'RE CRYING BECAUSE THE DAY'S ALMOST OVER.
COME NOW, DON'T WORRY, YOU'LL HAVE A CHANCE TO HAVE FUN TOMORROW, TOO!
I DON'T THINK SO. TOMORROW IS BACK-TO-SCHOOL!

A Missed Rendezvous

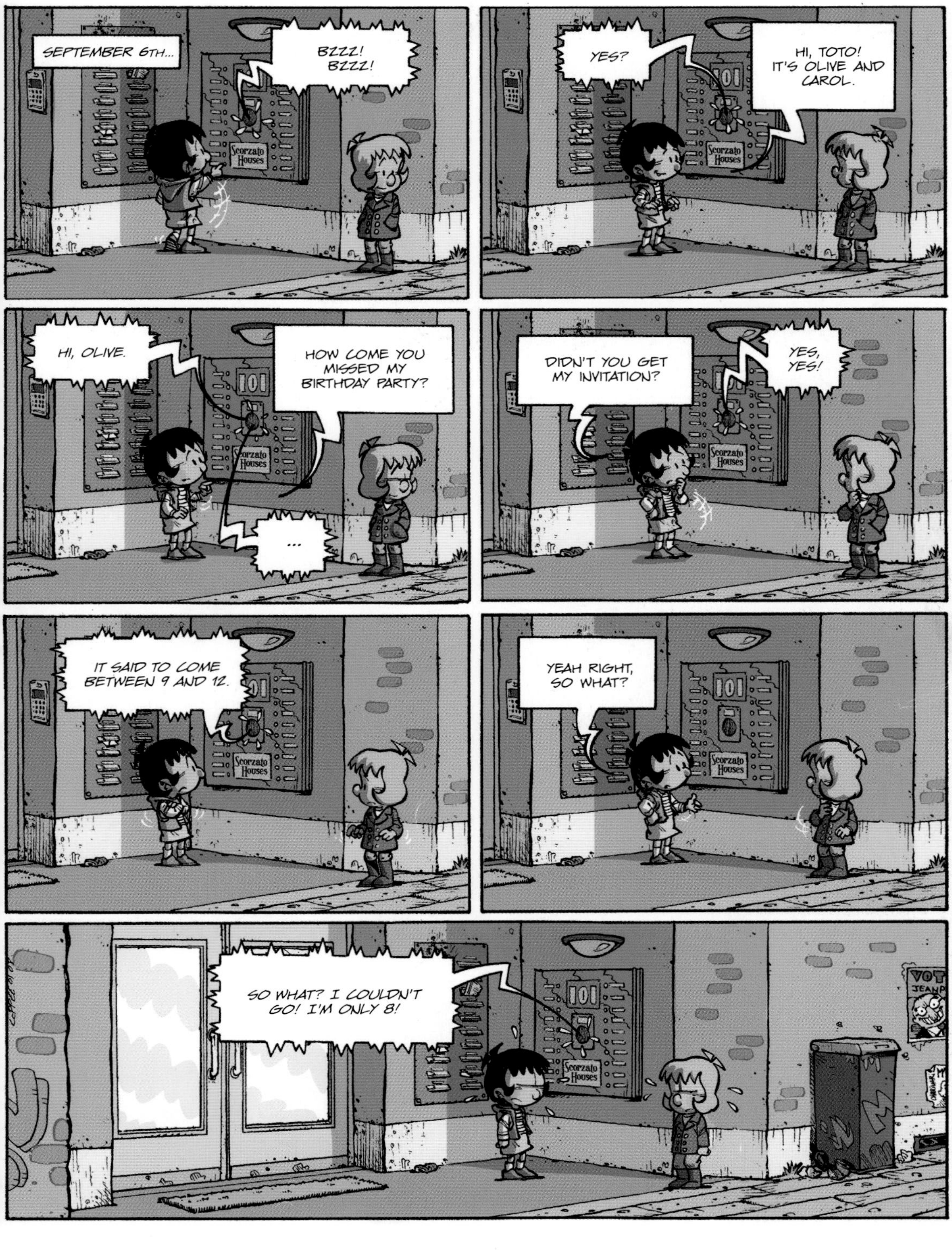
SEPTEMBER 6TH...
BZZZ! BZZZ!
YES?
HI, TOTO! IT'S OLIVE AND CAROL.
HI, OLIVE.
HOW COME YOU MISSED MY BIRTHDAY PARTY?
...
DIDN'T YOU GET MY INVITATION?
YES, YES!
IT SAID TO COME BETWEEN 9 AND 12.
YEAH RIGHT, SO WHAT?
SO WHAT? I COULDN'T GO! I'M ONLY 8!

A Watched Pot Never Boils

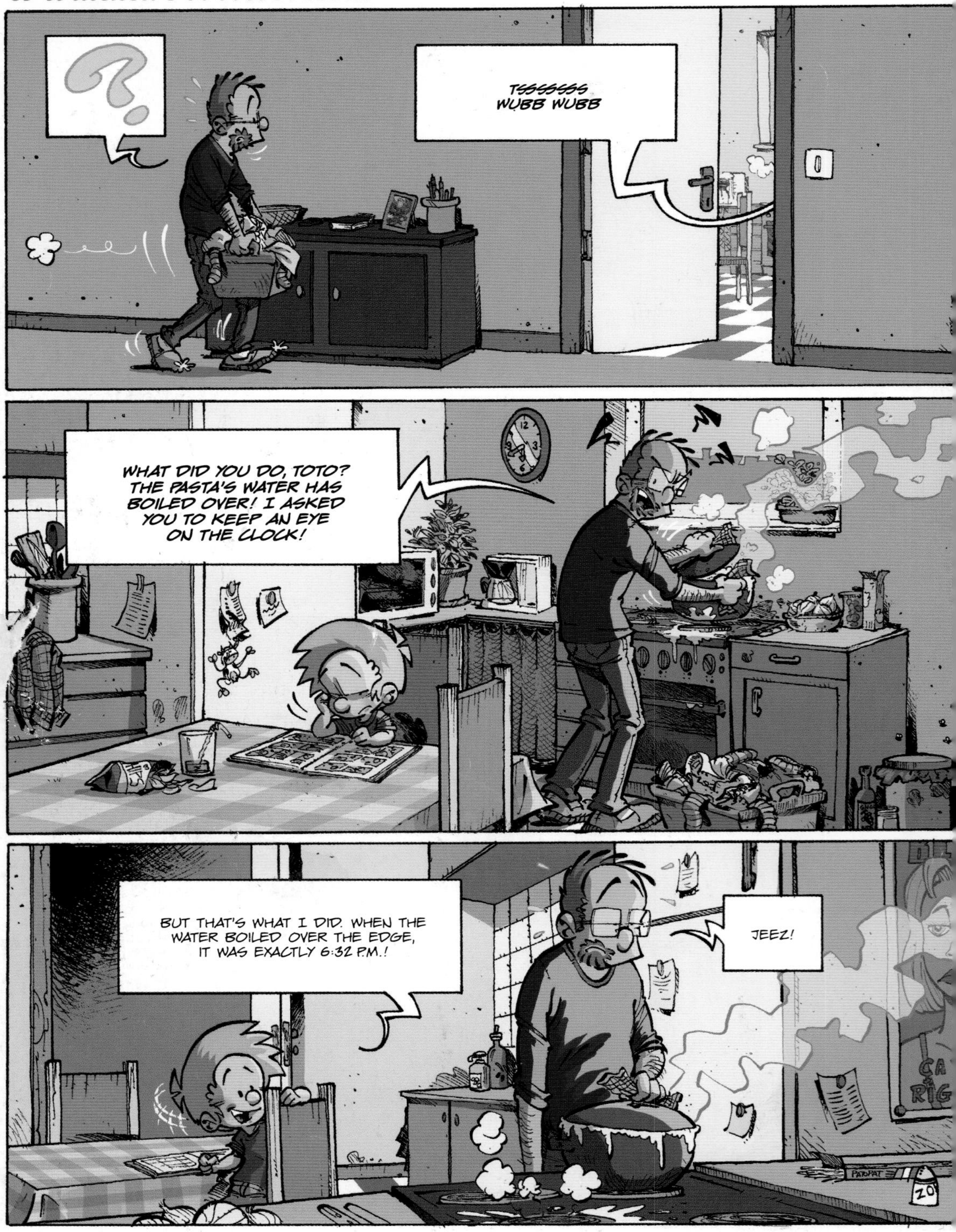
?
TSSSSSSS
WUBB WUBB
WHAT DID YOU DO, TOTO? THE PASTA'S WATER HAS BOILED OVER! I ASKED YOU TO KEEP AN EYE ON THE CLOCK!
BUT THAT'S WHAT I DID. WHEN THE WATER BOILED OVER THE EDGE, IT WAS EXACTLY 6:32 P.M.!
JEEZ!

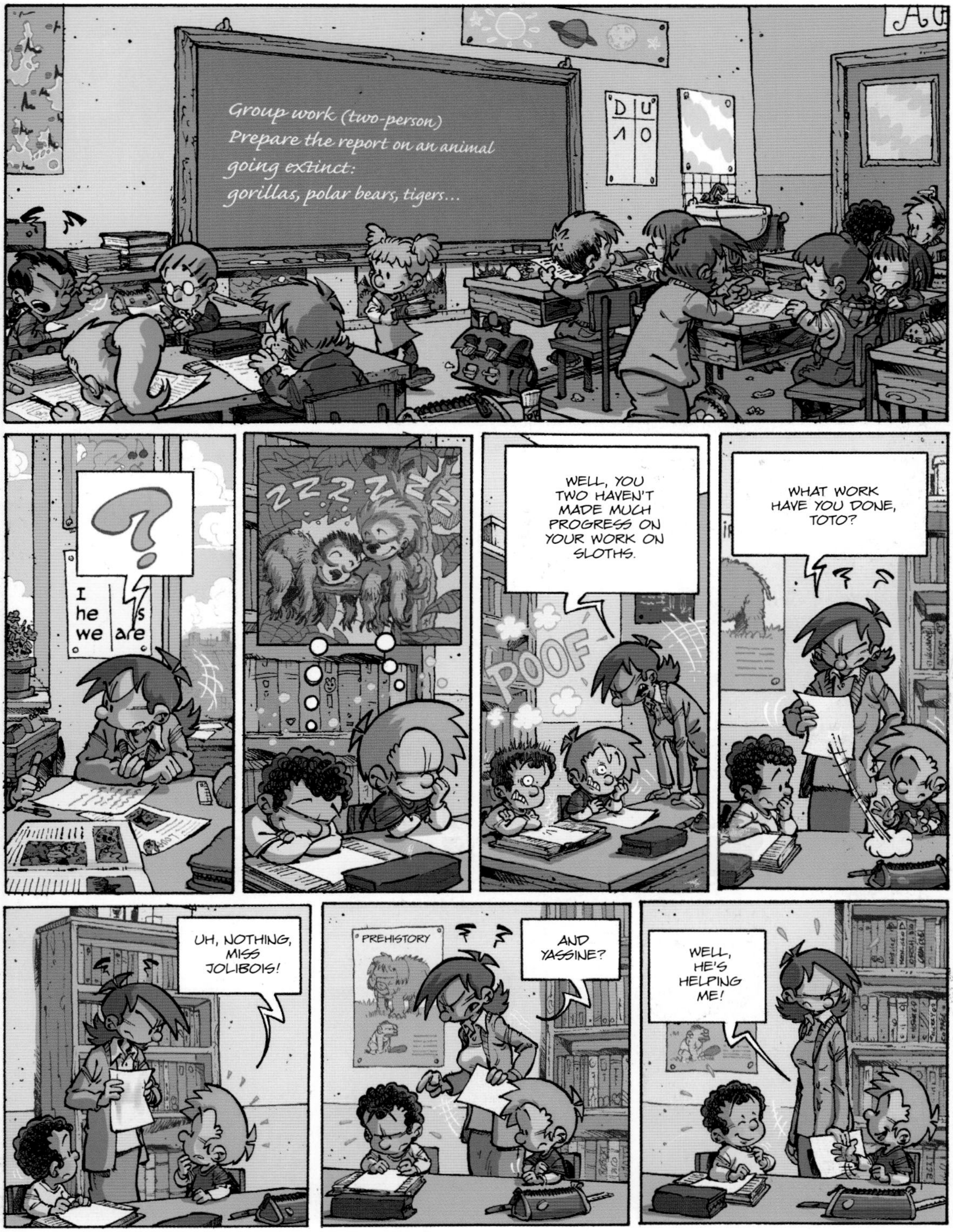
Group work (two-person)
Prepare the report on an animal going extinct:
gorillas, polar bears, tigers...
D U
1 0
?
I
he s
we are
ZZZZZZZ
WELL, YOU TWO HAVEN'T MADE MUCH PROGRESS ON YOUR WORK ON SLOTHS.
POOF
WHAT WORK HAVE YOU DONE, TOTO?
UH, NOTHING, MISS JOLIBOIS!
PREHISTORY
AND YASSINE?
WELL, HE'S HELPING ME!

All Things Come from Those Who Cough

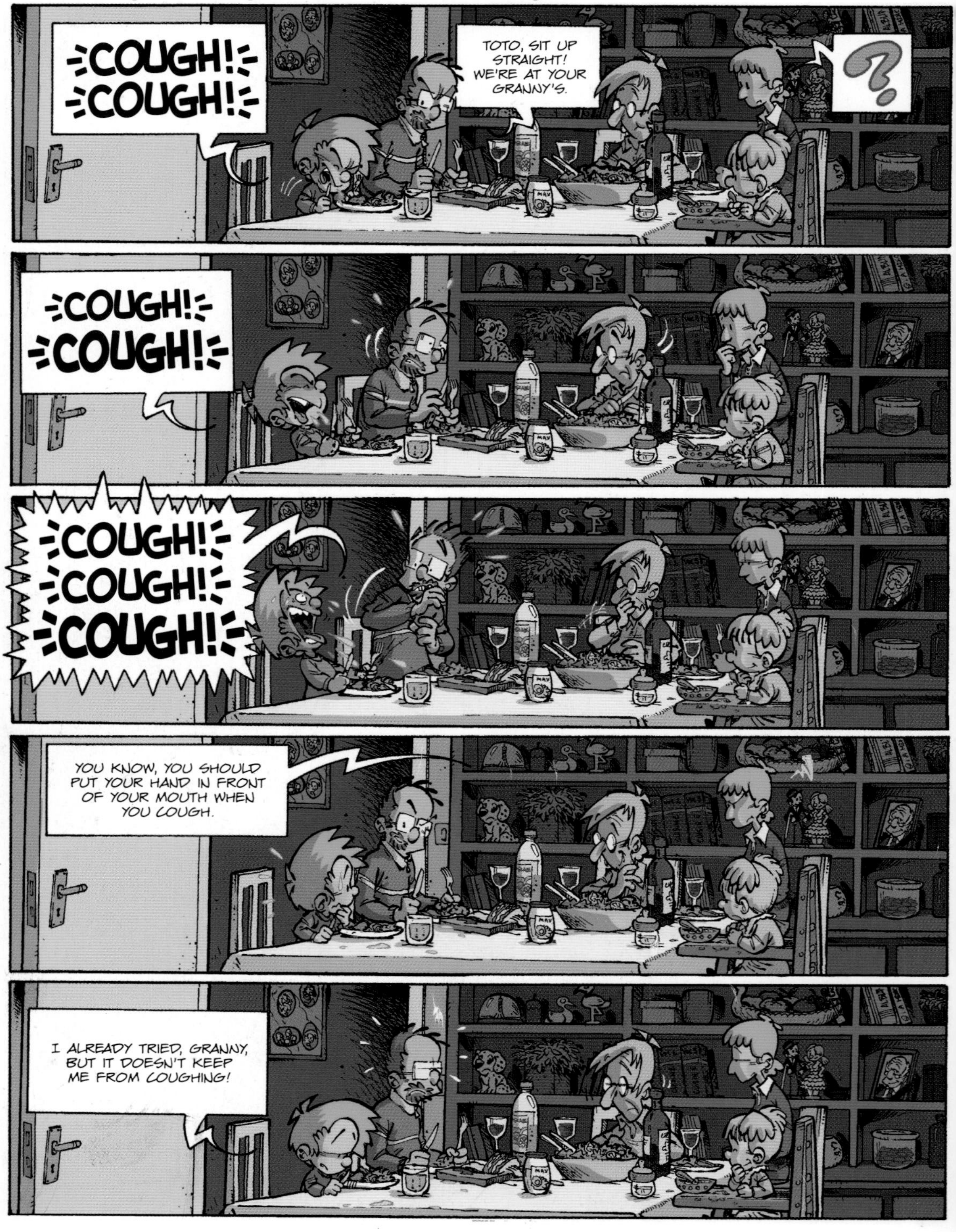
COUGH! COUGH!
TOTO, SIT UP STRAIGHT! WE'RE AT YOUR GRANNY'S.
?
COUGH! COUGH!
COUGH! COUGH! COUGH!
YOU KNOW, YOU SHOULD PUT YOUR HAND IN FRONT OF YOUR MOUTH WHEN YOU COUGH.
I ALREADY TRIED, GRANNY, BUT IT DOESN'T KEEP ME FROM COUGHING!

Tastes of Ink

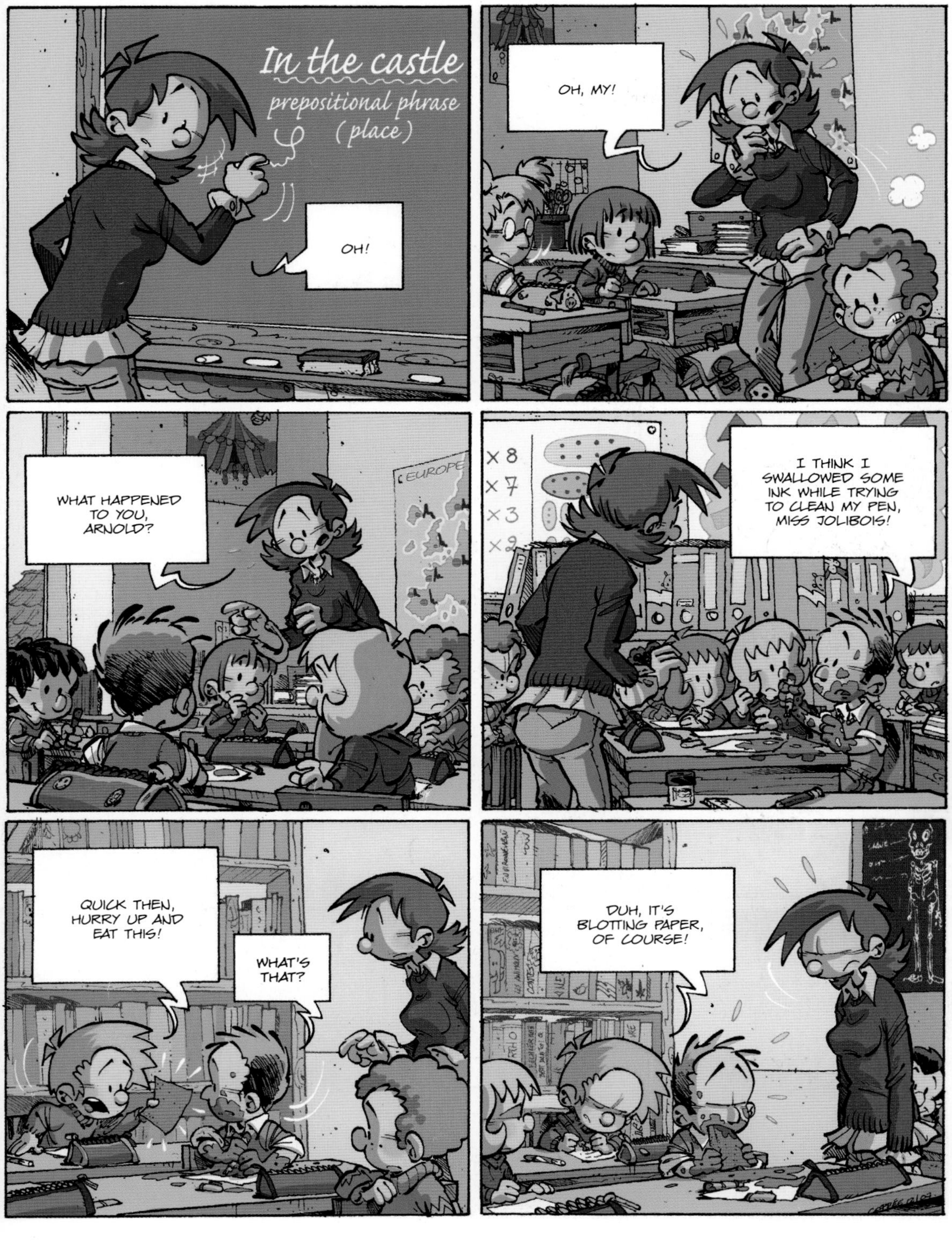
In the castle
prepositional phrase
(place)
OH!
OH, MY!
WHAT HAPPENED TO YOU, ARNOLD?
EUROPE
I THINK I SWALLOWED SOME INK WHILE TRYING TO CLEAN MY PEN, MISS JOLIBOIS!
QUICK THEN, HURRY UP AND EAT THIS!
WHAT'S THAT?
DUH, IT'S BLOTTING PAPER, OF COURSE!

A Down-to-Earth Answer

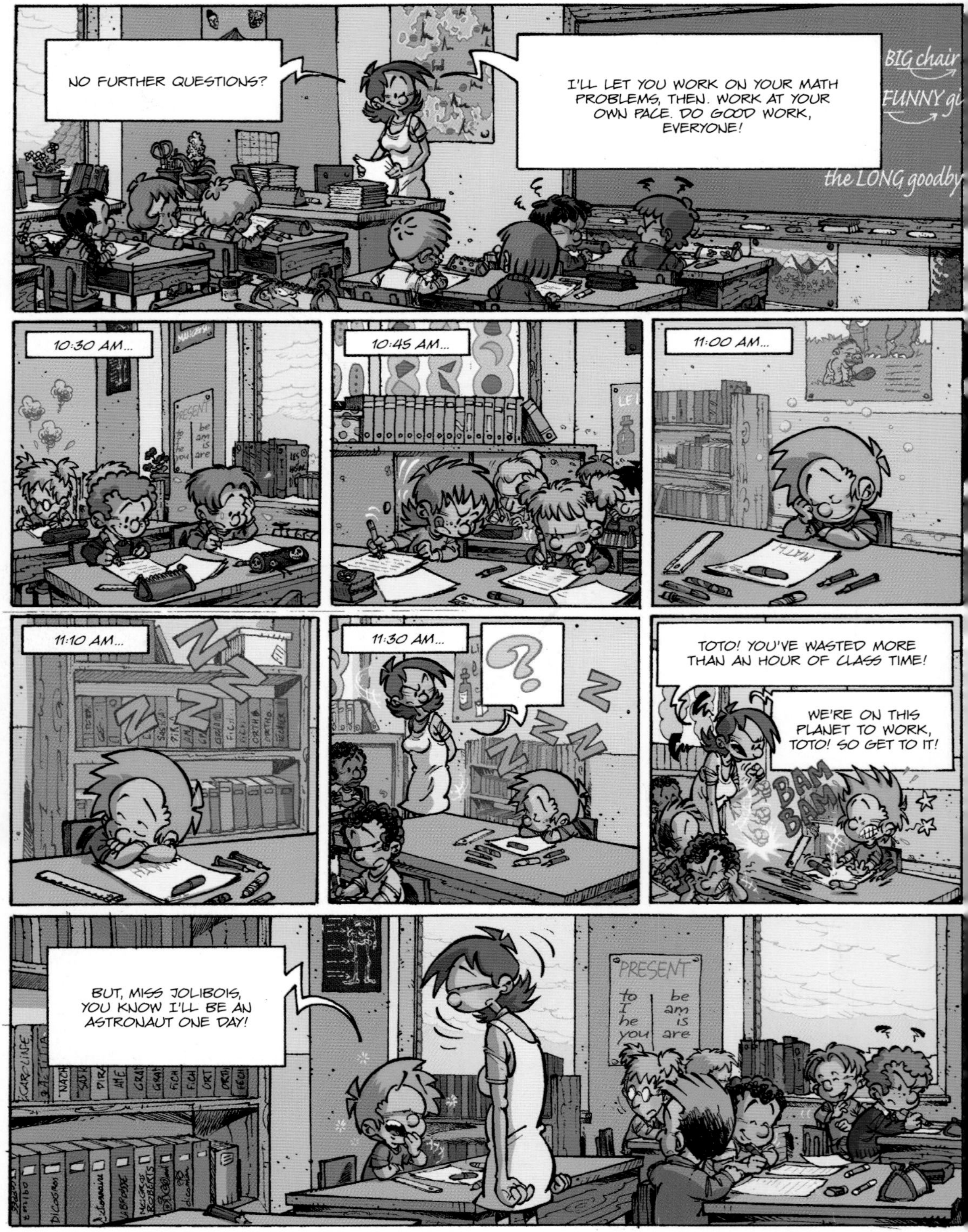
NO FURTHER QUESTIONS?
I'LL LET YOU WORK ON YOUR MATH PROBLEMS, THEN. WORK AT YOUR OWN PACE. DO GOOD WORK, EVERYONE!
10:30 AM...
10:45 AM...
11:00 AM...
11:10 AM...
11:30 AM...
?
TOTO! YOU'VE WASTED MORE THAN AN HOUR OF CLASS TIME!
WE'RE ON THIS PLANET TO WORK, TOTO! SO GET TO IT!
BAM BAM
BUT, MISS JOLIBOIS, YOU KNOW I'LL BE AN ASTRONAUT ONE DAY!

Hockey-K.O.

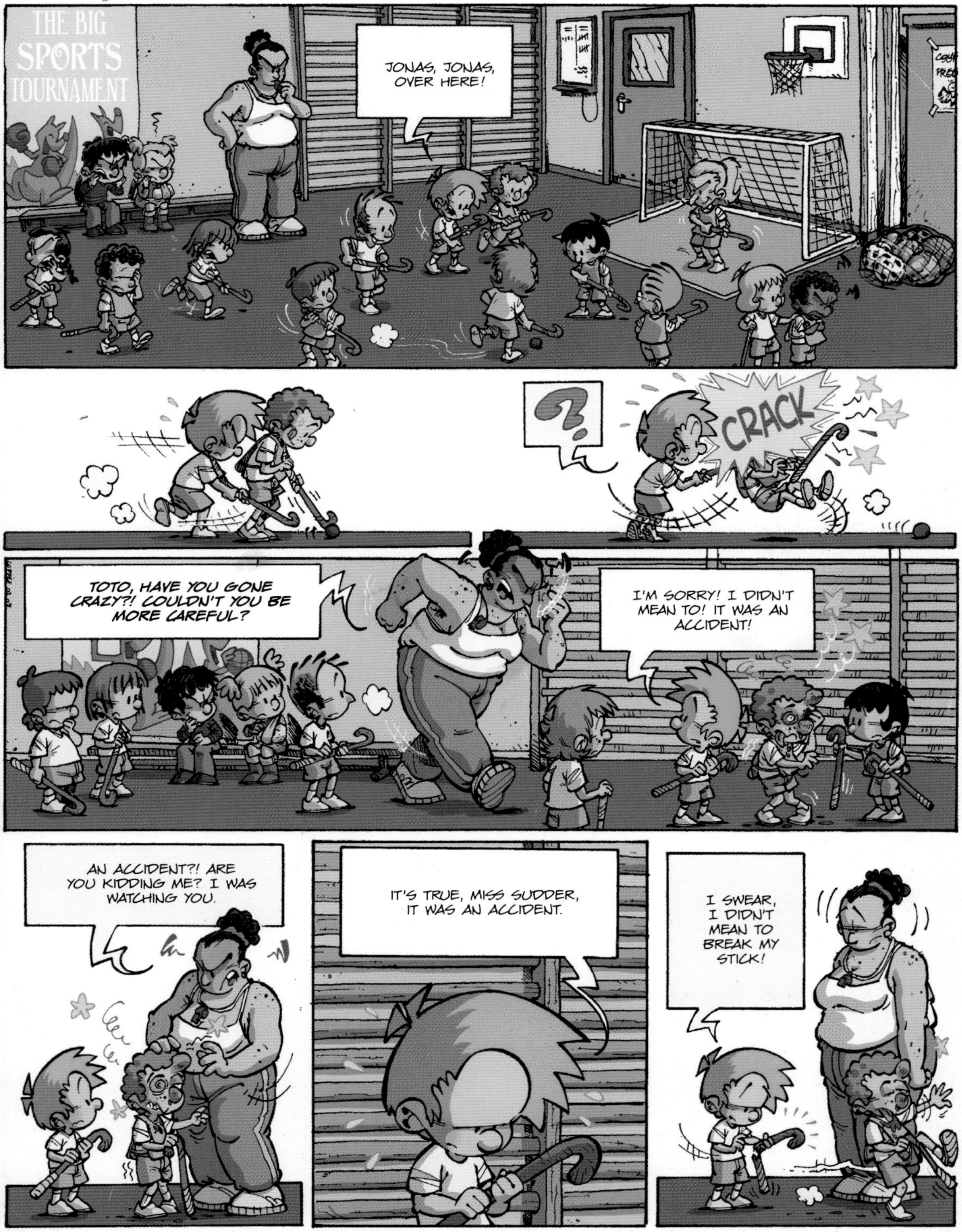
THE BIG SPORTS TOURNAMENT
JONAS, JONAS, OVER HERE!
?
CRACK
TOTO, HAVE YOU GONE CRAZY?! COULDN'T YOU BE MORE CAREFUL?
I'M SORRY! I DIDN'T MEAN TO! IT WAS AN ACCIDENT!
AN ACCIDENT?! ARE YOU KIDDING ME? I WAS WATCHING YOU.
IT'S TRUE, MISS SUDDER, IT WAS AN ACCIDENT.
I SWEAR, I DIDN'T MEAN TO BREAK MY STICK!

Public Service

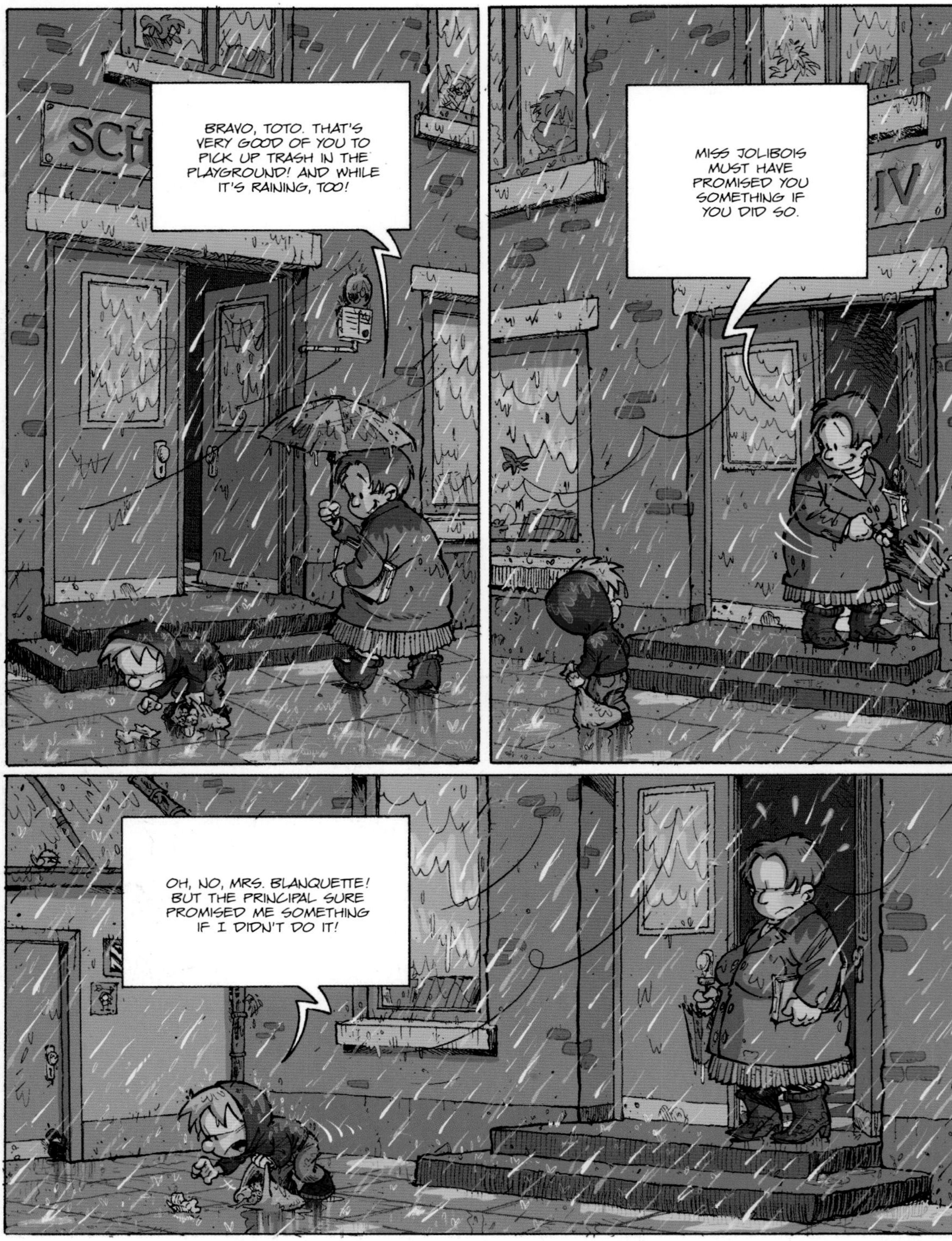
BRAVO, TOTO. THAT'S VERY GOOD OF YOU TO PICK UP TRASH IN THE PLAYGROUND! AND WHILE IT'S RAINING, TOO!
MISS JOLIBOIS MUST HAVE PROMISED YOU SOMETHING IF YOU DID SO.
OH, NO, MRS. BLANQUETTE! BUT THE PRINCIPAL SURE PROMISED ME SOMETHING IF I DIDN'T DO IT!

Tattletail!

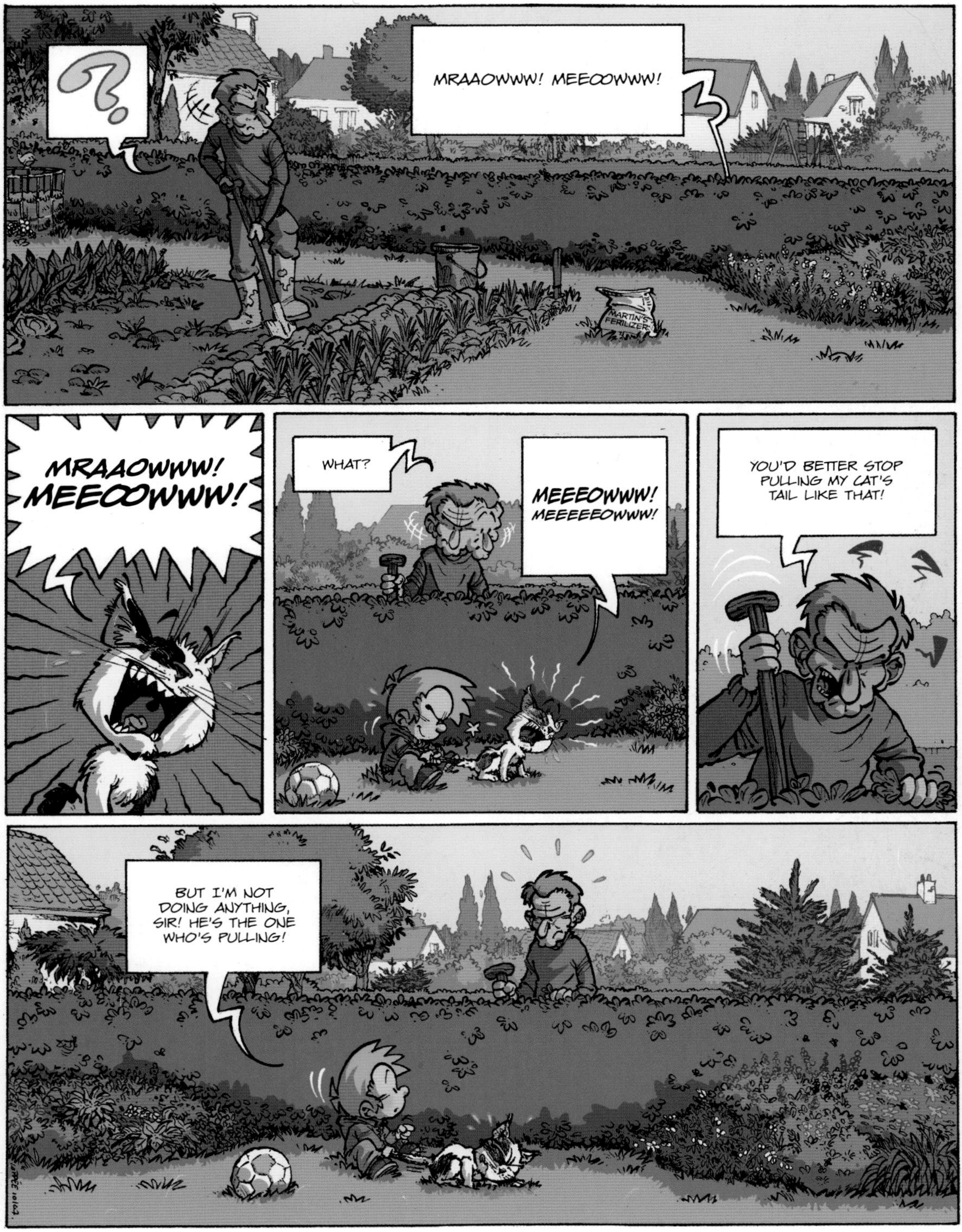
?
MRAAOWWW! MEEOOWWW!
MARTIN'S FERILIZER
MRAAOWWW! MEEOOWWW!
WHAT?
MEEEOWWW! MEEEEEOWWW!
YOU'D BETTER STOP PULLING MY CAT'S TAIL LIKE THAT!
BUT I'M NOT DOING ANYTHING, SIR! HE'S THE ONE WHO'S PULLING!

Goal!

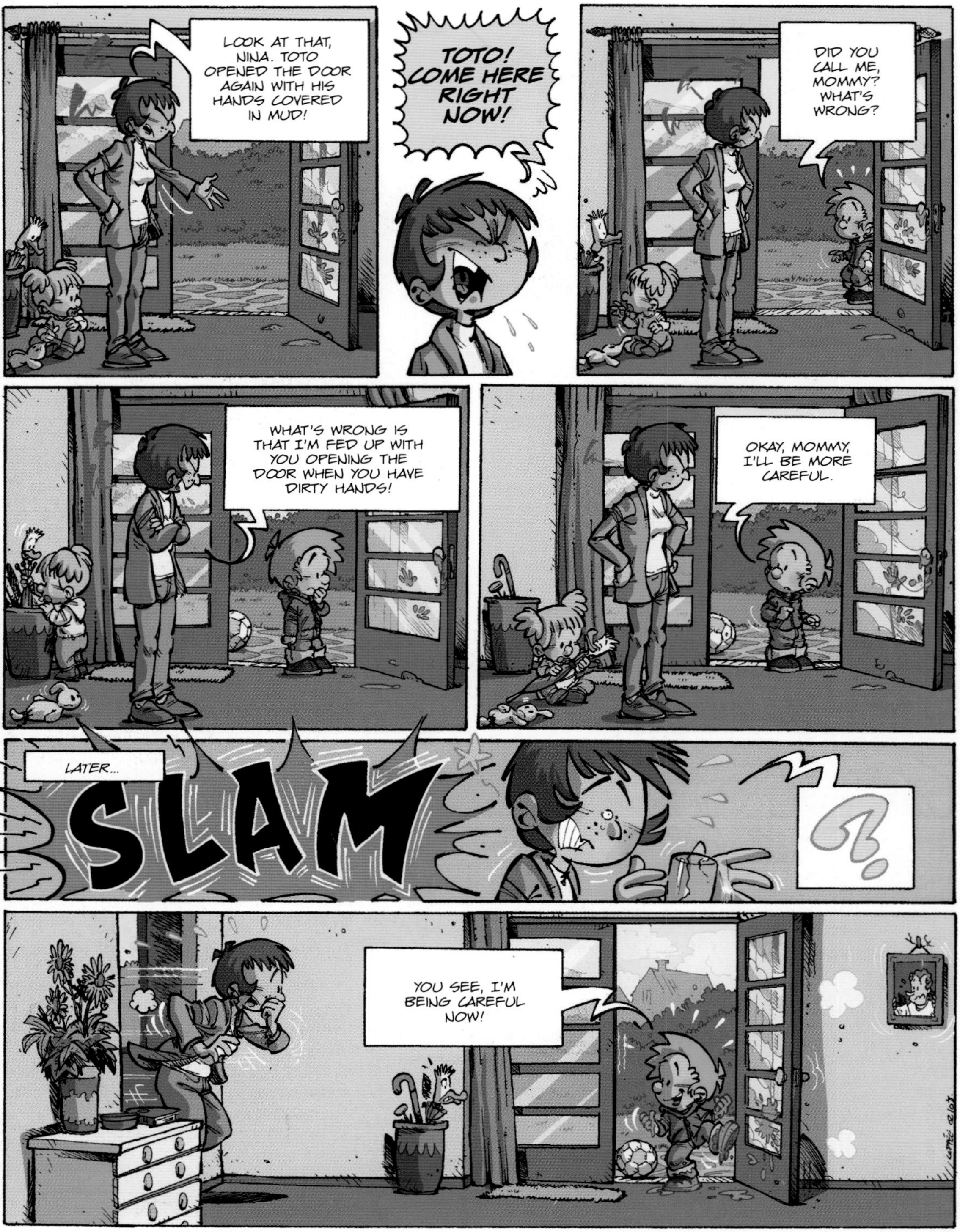

LOOK AT THAT, NINA. TOTO OPENED THE DOOR AGAIN WITH HIS HANDS COVERED IN MUD!
TOTO! COME HERE RIGHT NOW!
DID YOU CALL ME, MOMMY? WHAT'S WRONG?
WHAT'S WRONG IS THAT I'M FED UP WITH YOU OPENING THE DOOR WHEN YOU HAVE DIRTY HANDS!
OKAY, MOMMY, I'LL BE MORE CAREFUL.
LATER...
SLAM
?
YOU SEE, I'M BEING CAREFUL NOW!

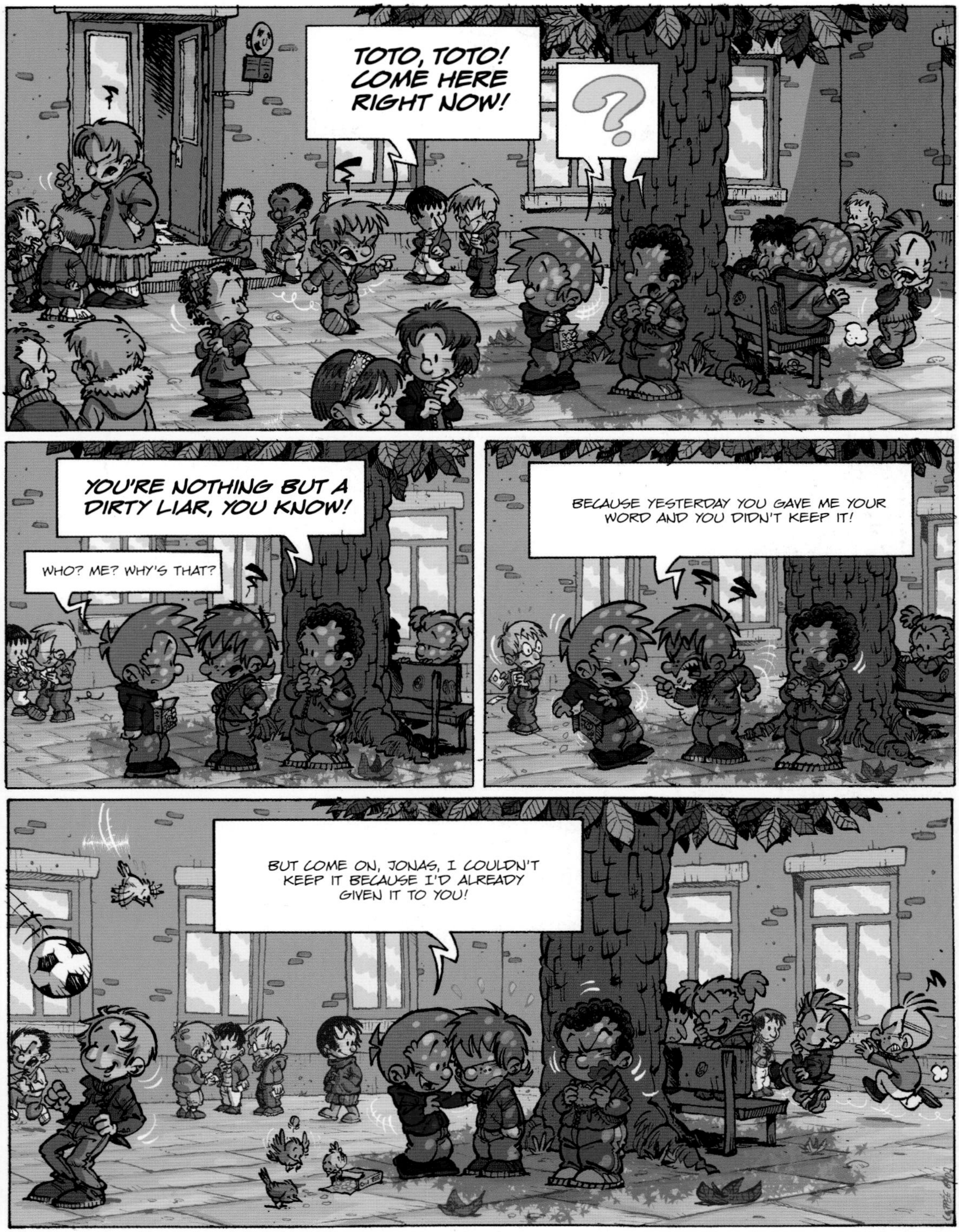
TOTO, TOTO! COME HERE RIGHT NOW!
?
YOU'RE NOTHING BUT A DIRTY LIAR, YOU KNOW!
WHO? ME? WHY'S THAT?
BECAUSE YESTERDAY YOU GAVE ME YOUR WORD AND YOU DIDN'T KEEP IT!
BUT COME ON, JONAS, I COULDN'T KEEP IT BECAUSE I'D ALREADY GIVEN IT TO YOU!

A Glass Half Full

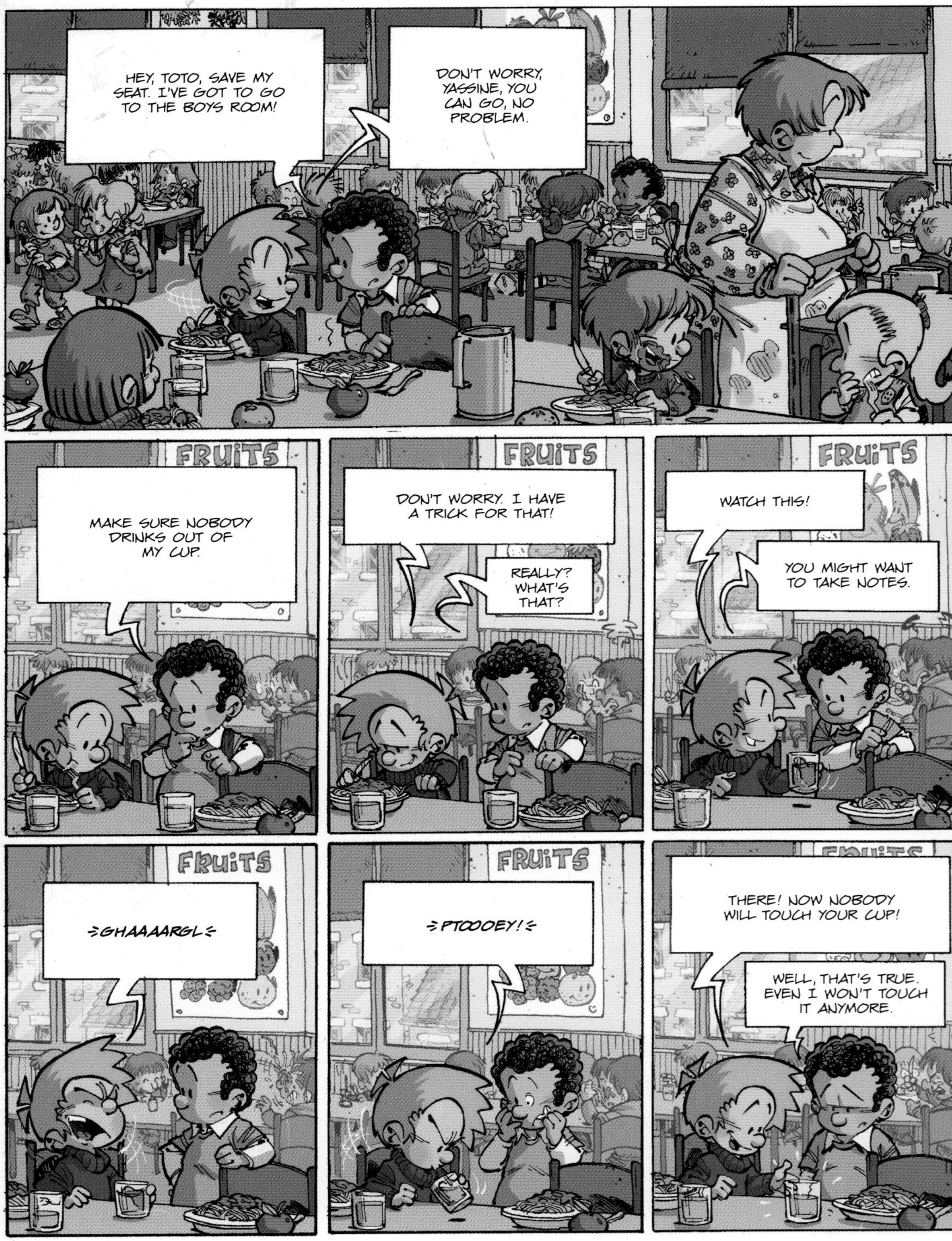
HEY, TOTO, SAVE MY SEAT. I'VE GOT TO GO TO THE BOYS ROOM!
DON'T WORRY, YASSINE, YOU CAN GO, NO PROBLEM.
MAKE SURE NOBODY DRINKS OUT OF MY CUP.
FRUITS
DON'T WORRY. I HAVE A TRICK FOR THAT!
REALLY? WHAT'S THAT?
WATCH THIS!
YOU MIGHT WANT TO TAKE NOTES.
GHAAAARGL
PTOOOEY!
THERE! NOW NOBODY WILL TOUCH YOUR CUP!
WELL, THAT'S TRUE. EVEN I WON'T TOUCH IT ANYMORE.

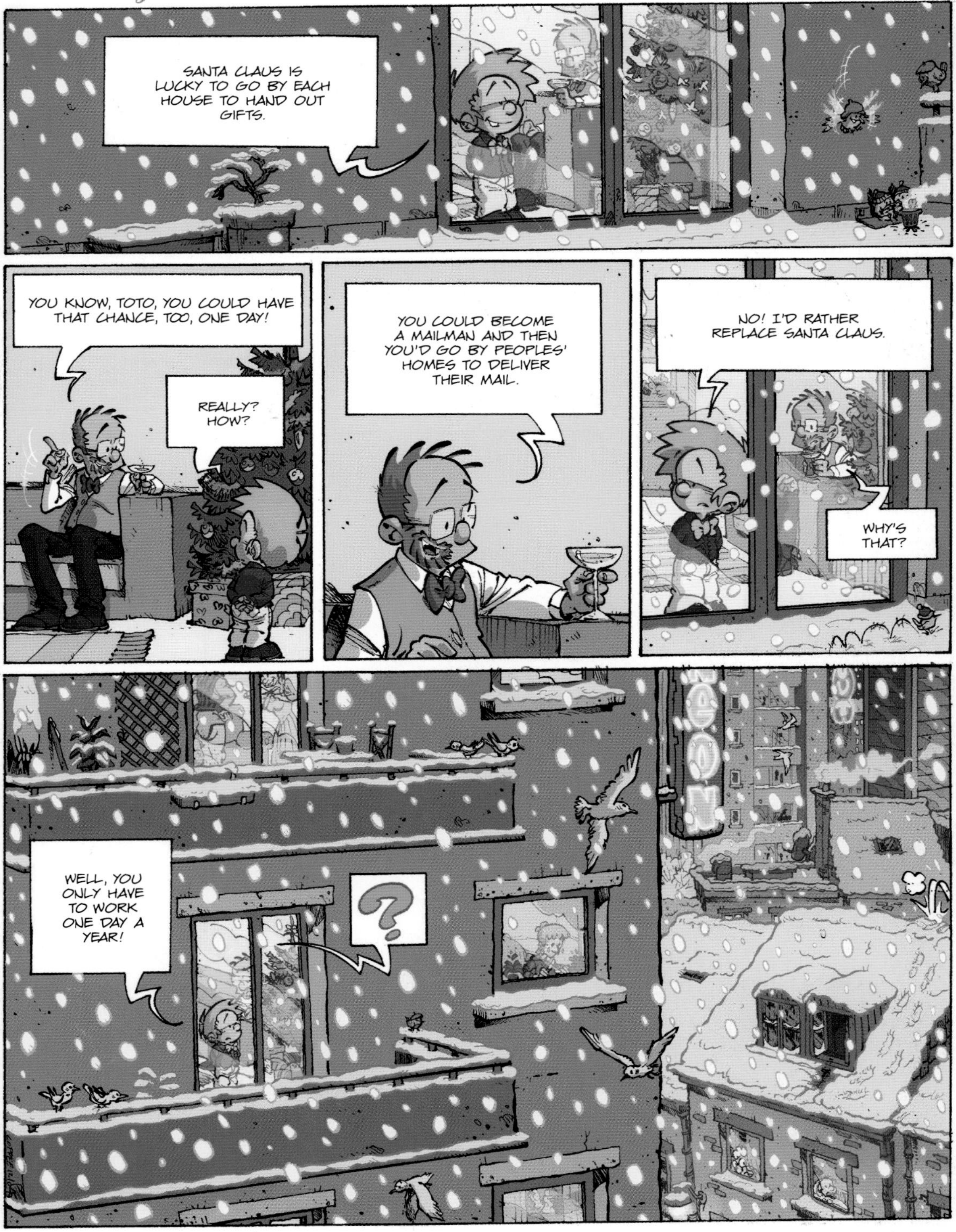
SANTA CLAUS IS LUCKY TO GO BY EACH HOUSE TO HAND OUT GIFTS.
YOU KNOW, TOTO, YOU COULD HAVE THAT CHANCE, TOO, ONE DAY!
REALLY? HOW?
YOU COULD BECOME A MAILMAN AND THEN YOU'D GO BY PEOPLES' HOMES TO DELIVER THEIR MAIL.
NO! I'D RATHER REPLACE SANTA CLAUS.
WHY'S THAT?
WELL, YOU ONLY HAVE TO WORK ONE DAY A YEAR!
?

Counting Biases

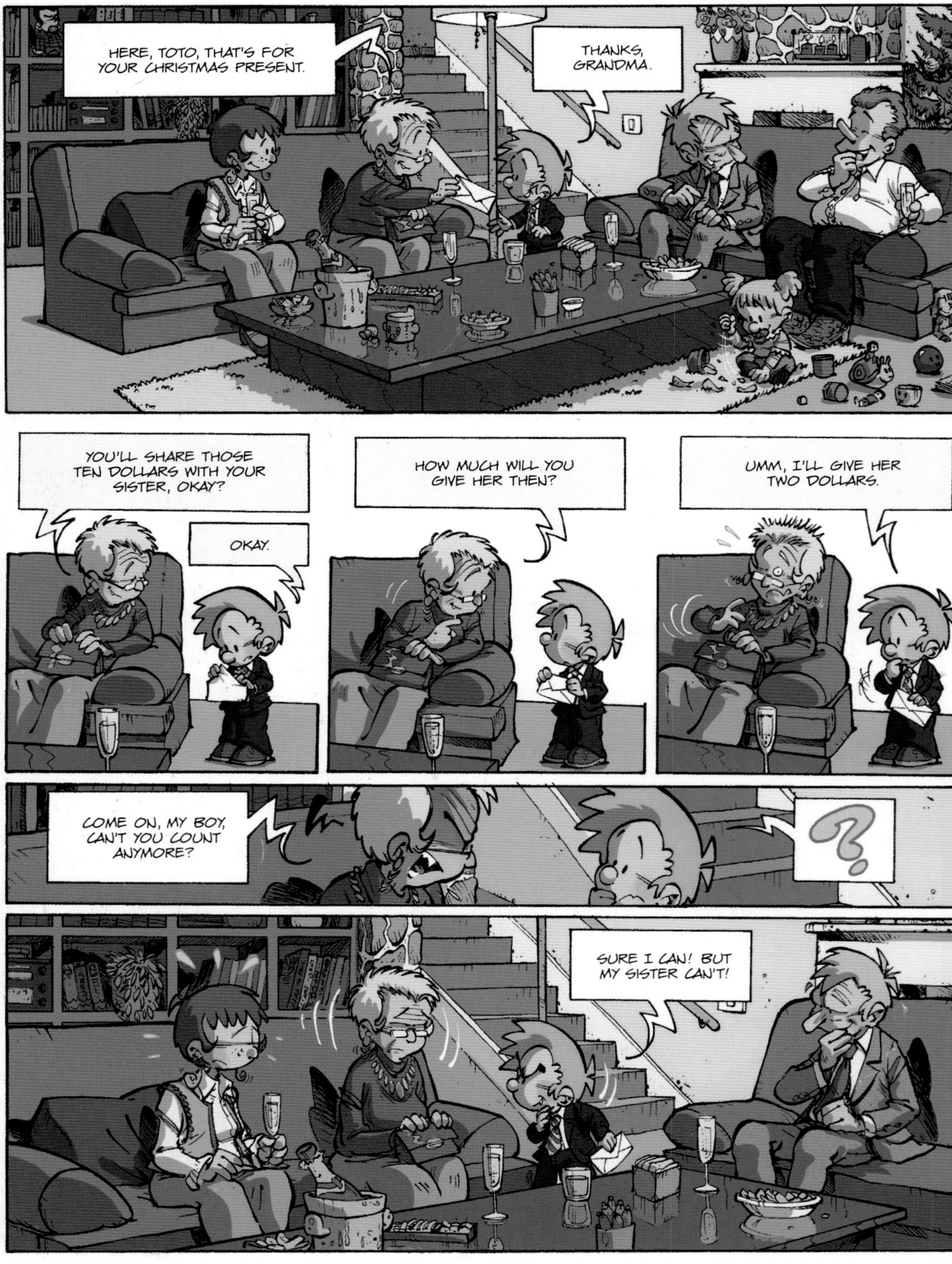

HERE, TOTO, THAT'S FOR YOUR CHRISTMAS PRESENT.
THANKS, GRANDMA.
YOU'LL SHARE THOSE TEN DOLLARS WITH YOUR SISTER, OKAY?
OKAY.
HOW MUCH WILL YOU GIVE HER THEN?
UMM, I'LL GIVE HER TWO DOLLARS.
COME ON, MY BOY, CAN'T YOU COUNT ANYMORE?
?
SURE I CAN! BUT MY SISTER CAN'T!

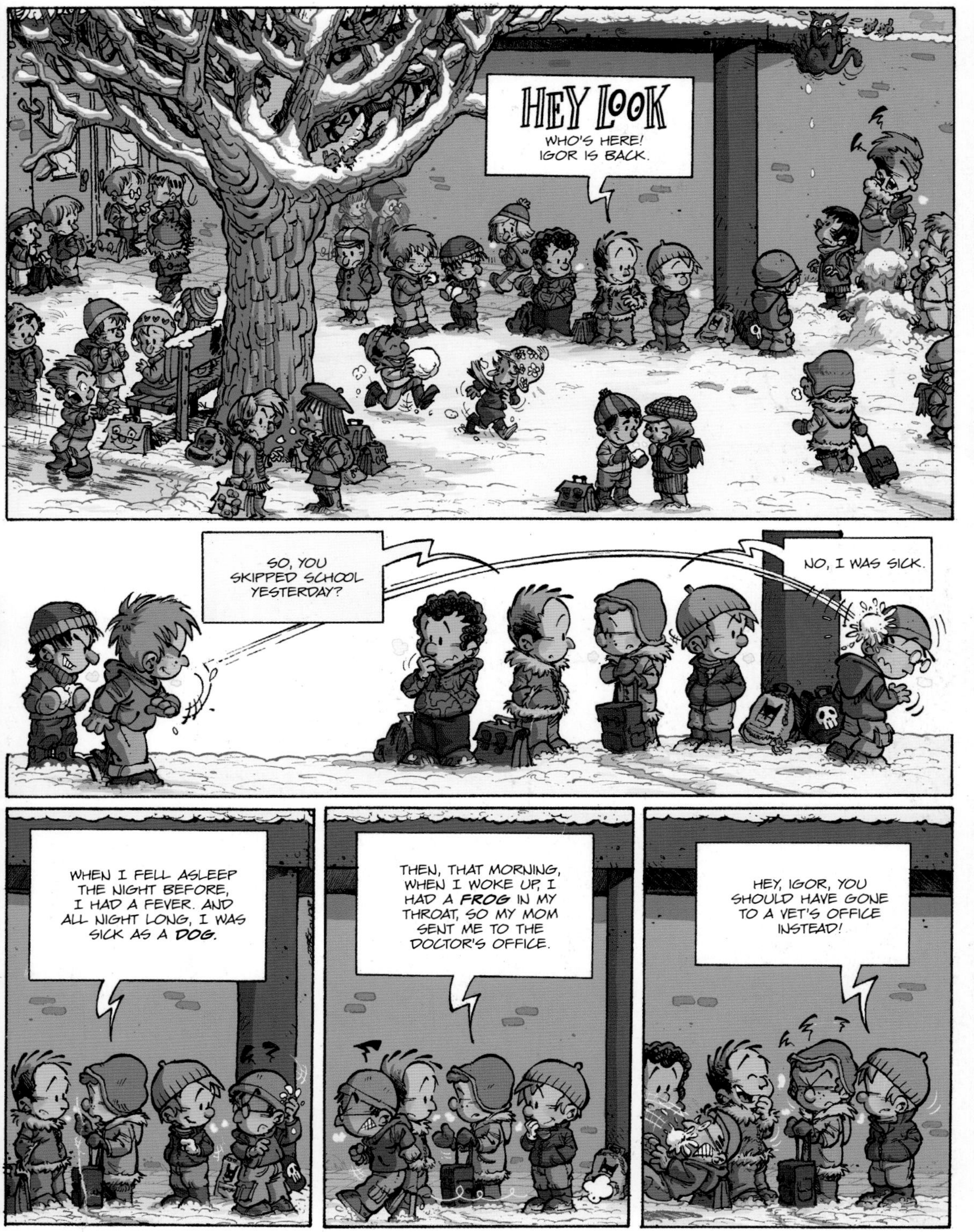
HEY LOOK
WHO'S HERE! IGOR IS BACK.
SO, YOU SKIPPED SCHOOL YESTERDAY?
NO, I WAS SICK.
WHEN I FELL ASLEEP THE NIGHT BEFORE, I HAD A FEVER. AND ALL NIGHT LONG, I WAS SICK AS A DOG.
THEN, THAT MORNING, WHEN I WOKE UP, I HAD A FROG IN MY THROAT, SO MY MOM SENT ME TO THE DOCTOR'S OFFICE.
HEY, IGOR, YOU SHOULD HAVE GONE TO A VET'S OFFICE INSTEAD!

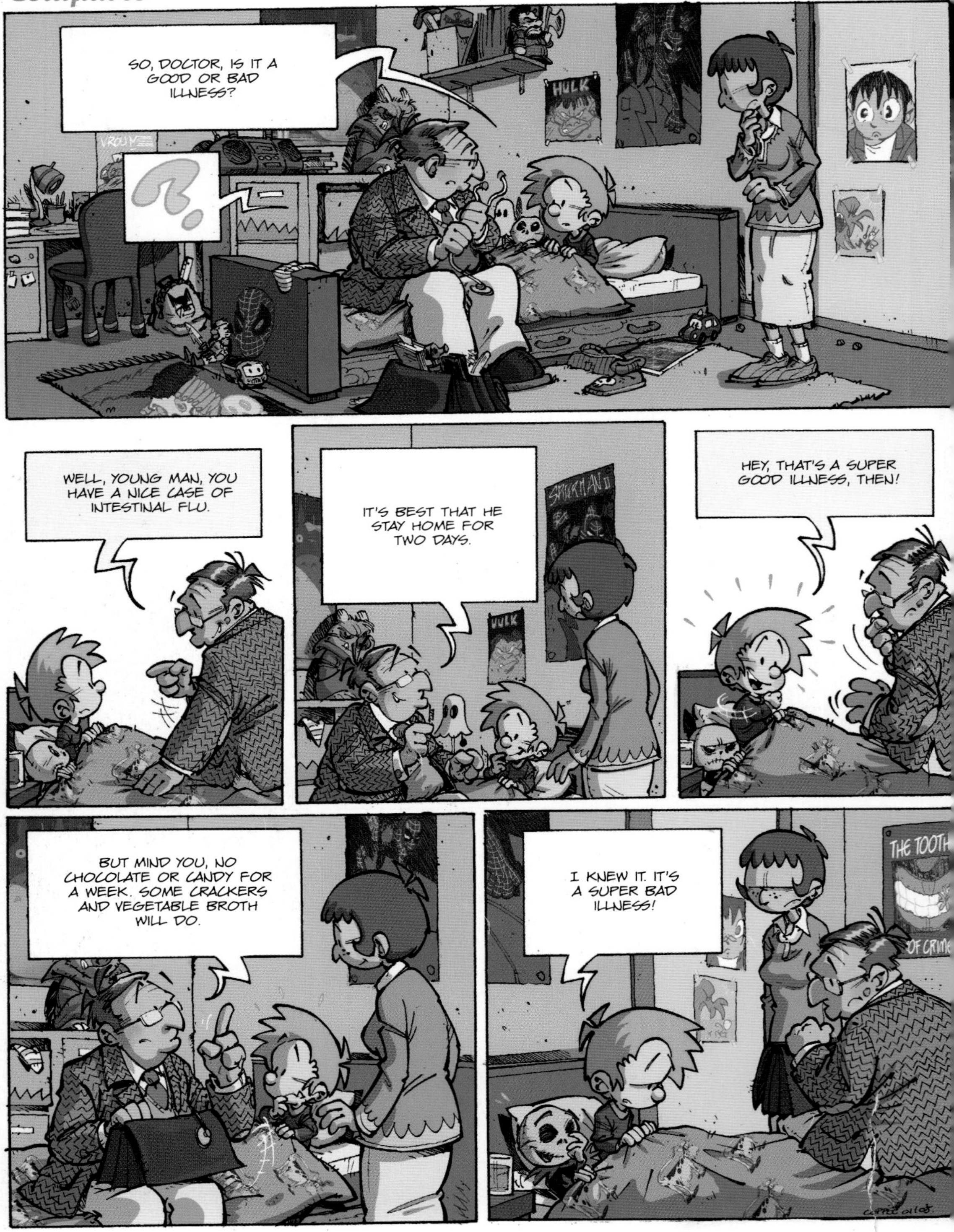
SO, DOCTOR, IS IT A GOOD OR BAD ILLNESS?
?
HULK
WELL, YOUNG MAN, YOU HAVE A NICE CASE OF INTESTINAL FLU.
IT'S BEST THAT HE STAY HOME FOR TWO DAYS.
HULK
HEY, THAT'S A SUPER GOOD ILLNESS, THEN!
BUT MIND YOU, NO CHOCOLATE OR CANDY FOR A WEEK. SOME CRACKERS AND VEGETABLE BROTH WILL DO.
I KNEW IT. IT'S A SUPER BAD ILLNESS!
THE TOOTH
OF CRIME

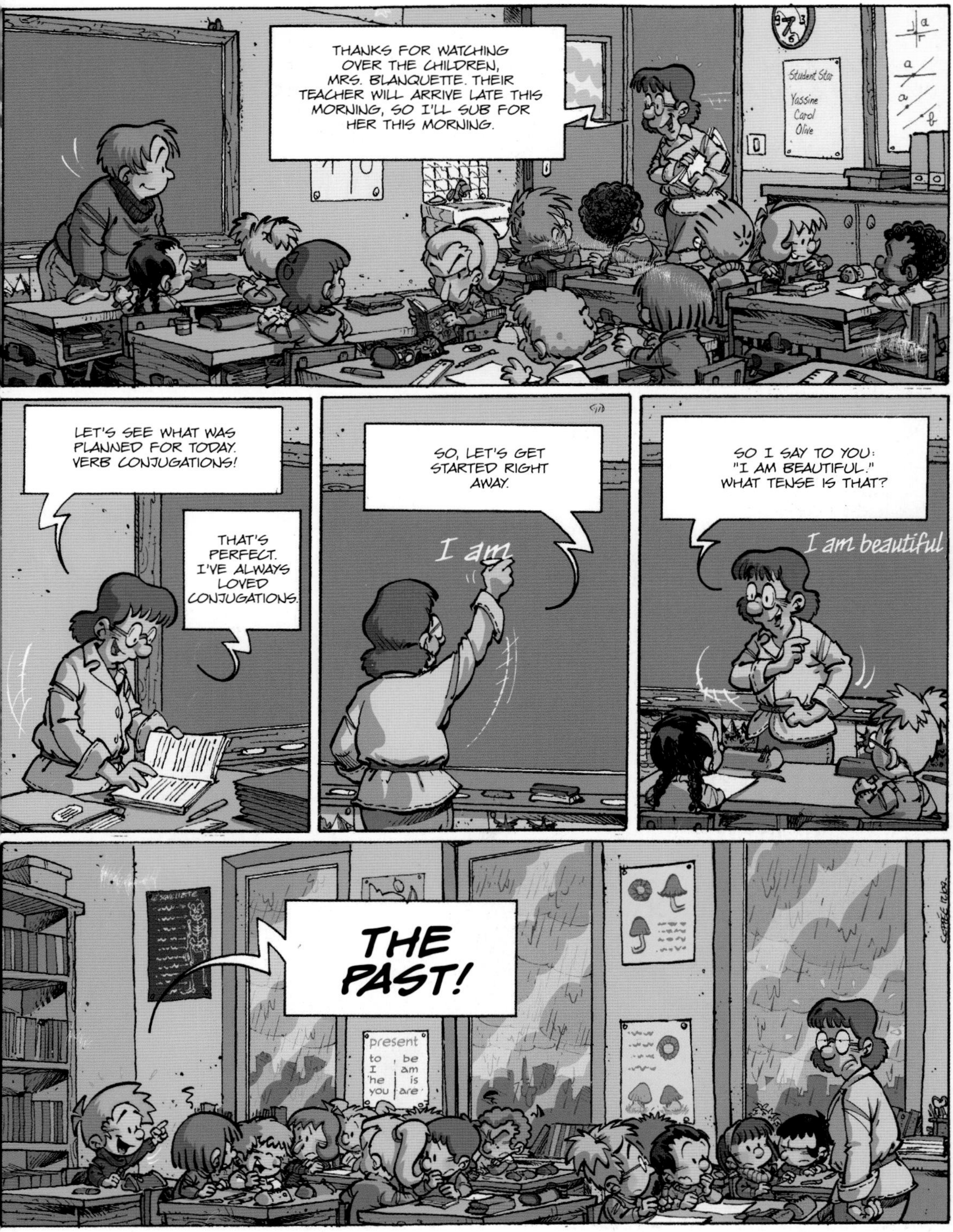
THANKS FOR WATCHING OVER THE CHILDREN, MRS. BLANQUETTE. THEIR TEACHER WILL ARRIVE LATE THIS MORNING, SO I'LL SUB FOR HER THIS MORNING.
Student Star
Yassine
Carol
Olive
LET'S SEE WHAT WAS PLANNED FOR TODAY. VERB CONJUGATIONS!
THAT'S PERFECT. I'VE ALWAYS LOVED CONJUGATIONS.
SO, LET'S GET STARTED RIGHT AWAY.
I am
SO I SAY TO YOU: "I AM BEAUTIFUL." WHAT TENSE IS THAT?
I am beautiful
THE PAST!
present
to be
I am
he is
you are

Bubbling Hot

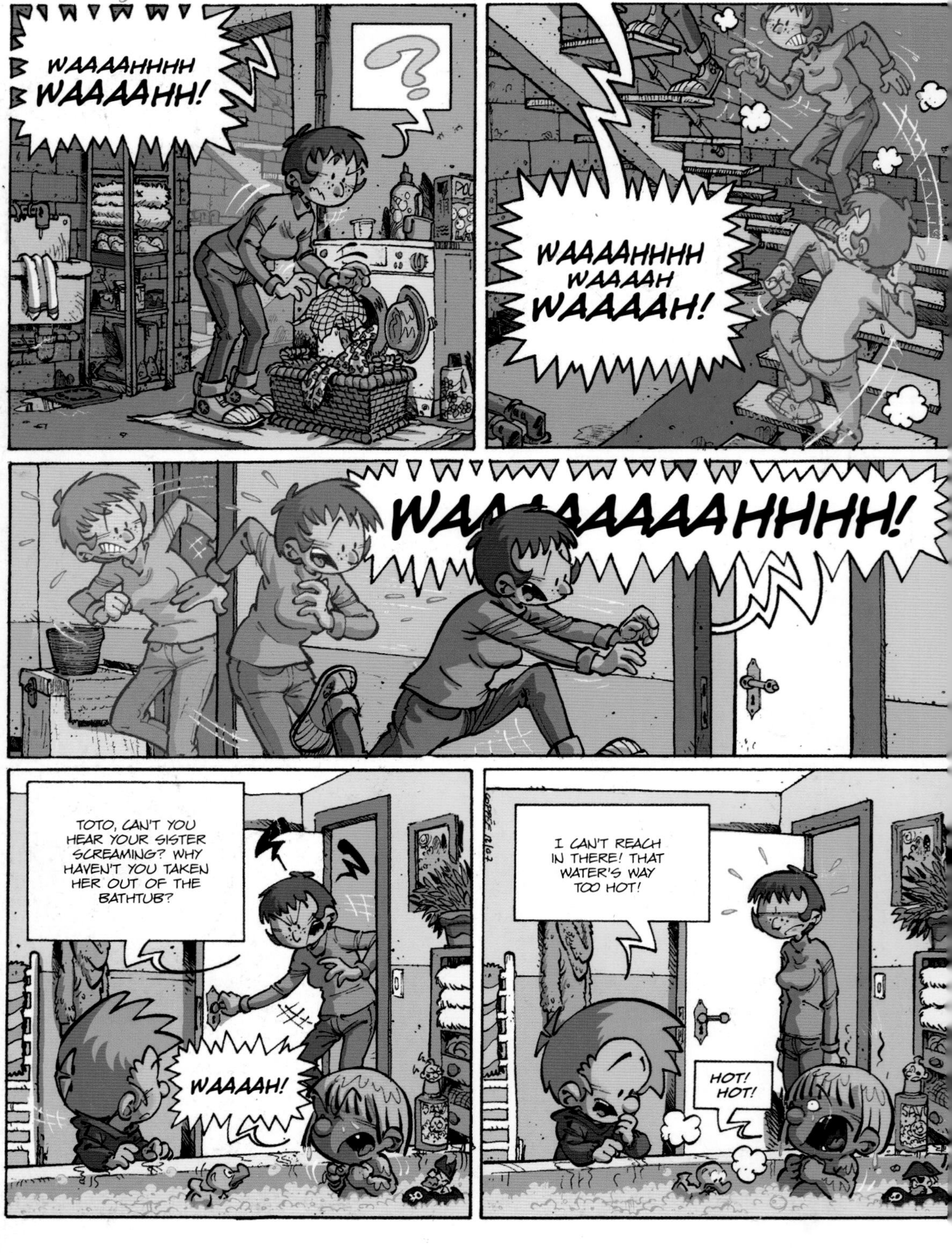

WAAAAHHHH WAAAAHH!
WAAAAHHHH WAAAAH WAAAAH!
WAAAAAAAAAHHHH!
TOTO, CAN'T YOU HEAR YOUR SISTER SCREAMING? WHY HAVEN'T YOU TAKEN HER OUT OF THE BATHTUB?
WAAAAH!
I CAN'T REACH IN THERE! THAT WATER'S WAY TOO HOT!
HOT! HOT!

A Slow Learner

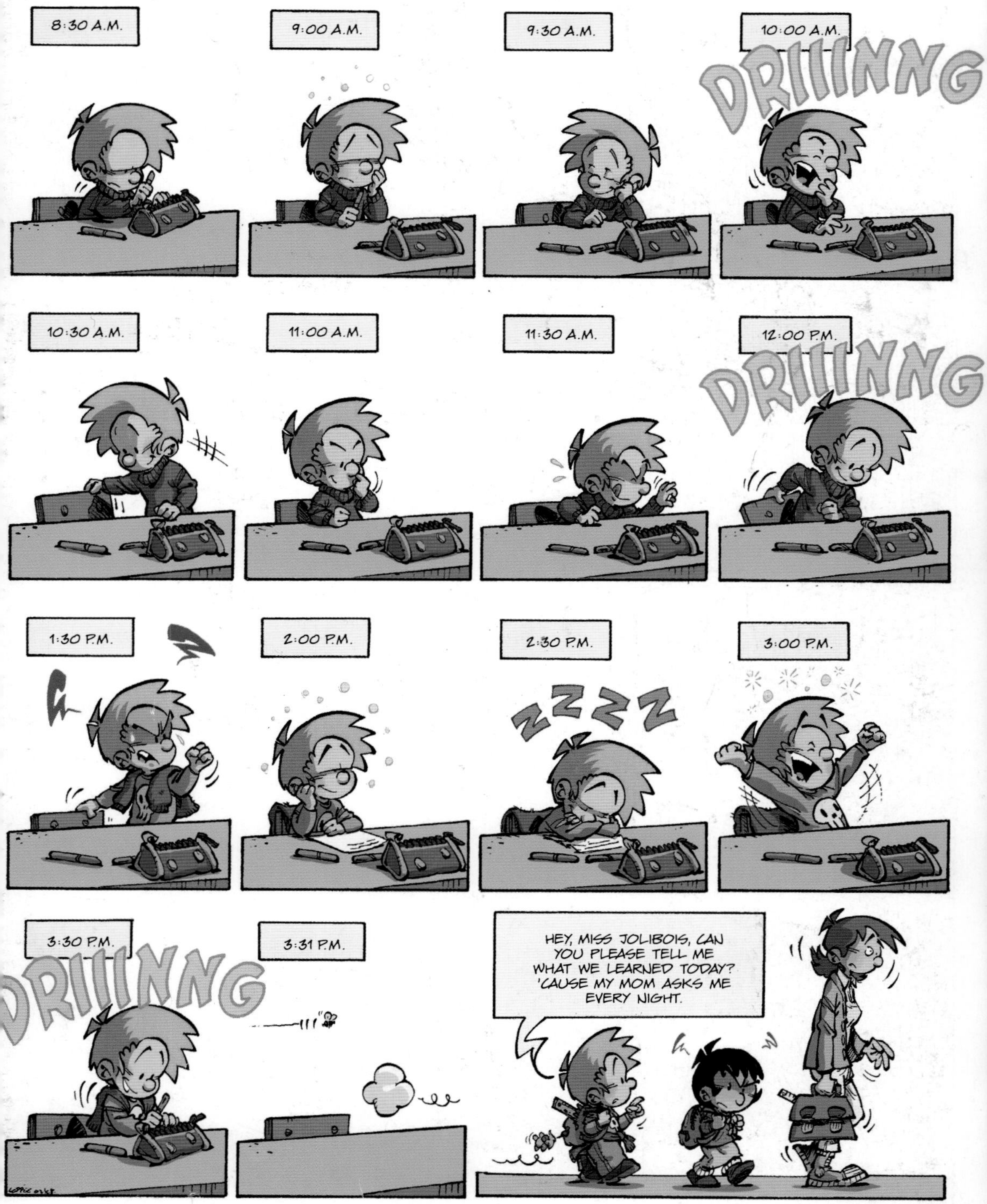
8:30 A.M.
9:00 A.M.
9:30 A.M.
10:00 A.M.
DRIIINNG
10:30 A.M.
11:00 A.M.
11:30 A.M.
12:00 P.M.
DRIIINNG
1:30 P.M.
2:00 P.M.
2:30 P.M.
ZZZZ
3:00 P.M.
3:30 P.M.
DRIIINNG
3:31 P.M.
HEY, MISS JOLIBOIS, CAN YOU PLEASE TELL ME WHAT WE LEARNED TODAY? 'CAUSE MY MOM ASKS ME EVERY NIGHT.

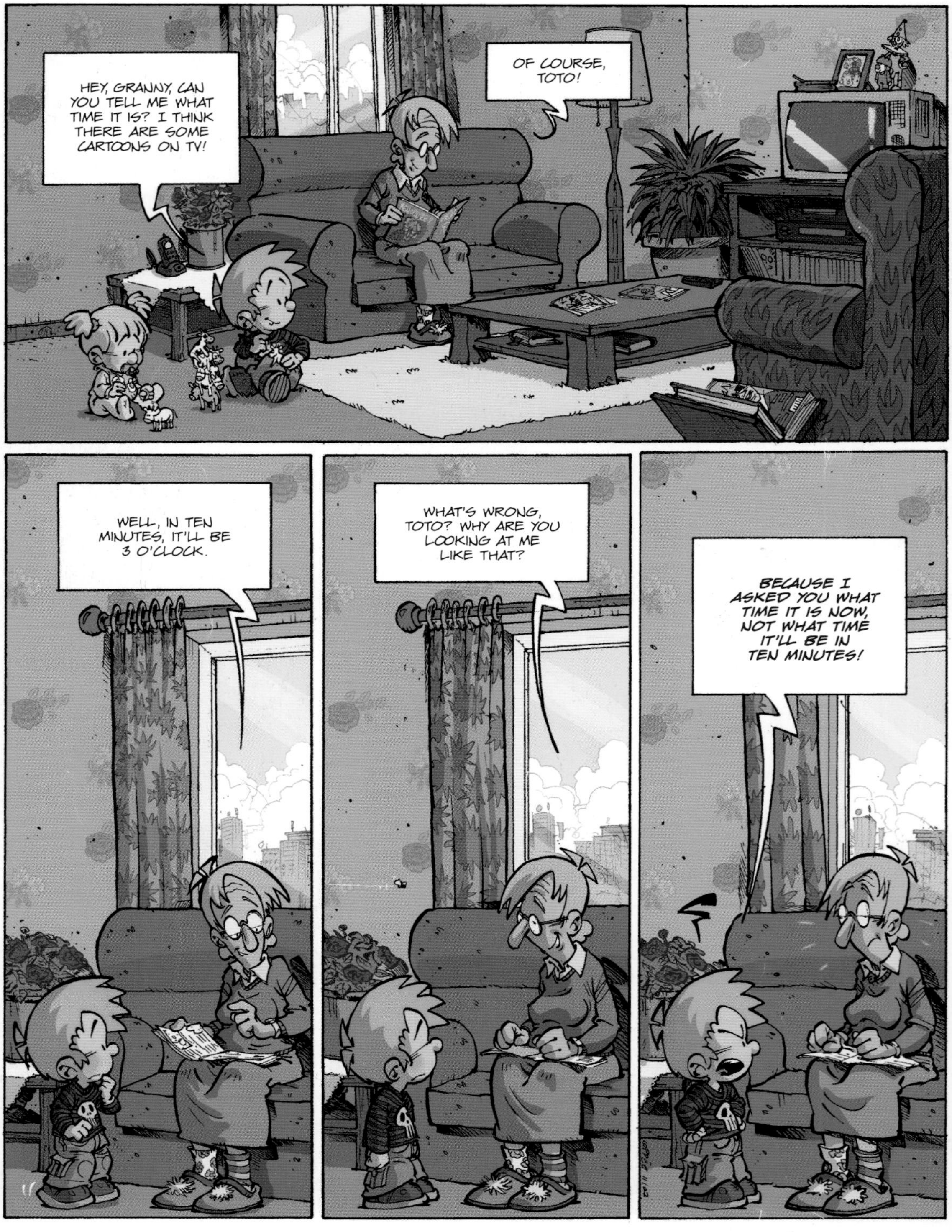

HEY, GRANNY, CAN YOU TELL ME WHAT TIME IT IS? I THINK THERE ARE SOME CARTOONS ON TV!
OF COURSE, TOTO!
WELL, IN TEN MINUTES, IT'LL BE 3 O'CLOCK.
WHAT'S WRONG, TOTO? WHY ARE YOU LOOKING AT ME LIKE THAT?
BECAUSE I ASKED YOU WHAT TIME IT IS NOW, NOT WHAT TIME IT'LL BE IN TEN MINUTES!

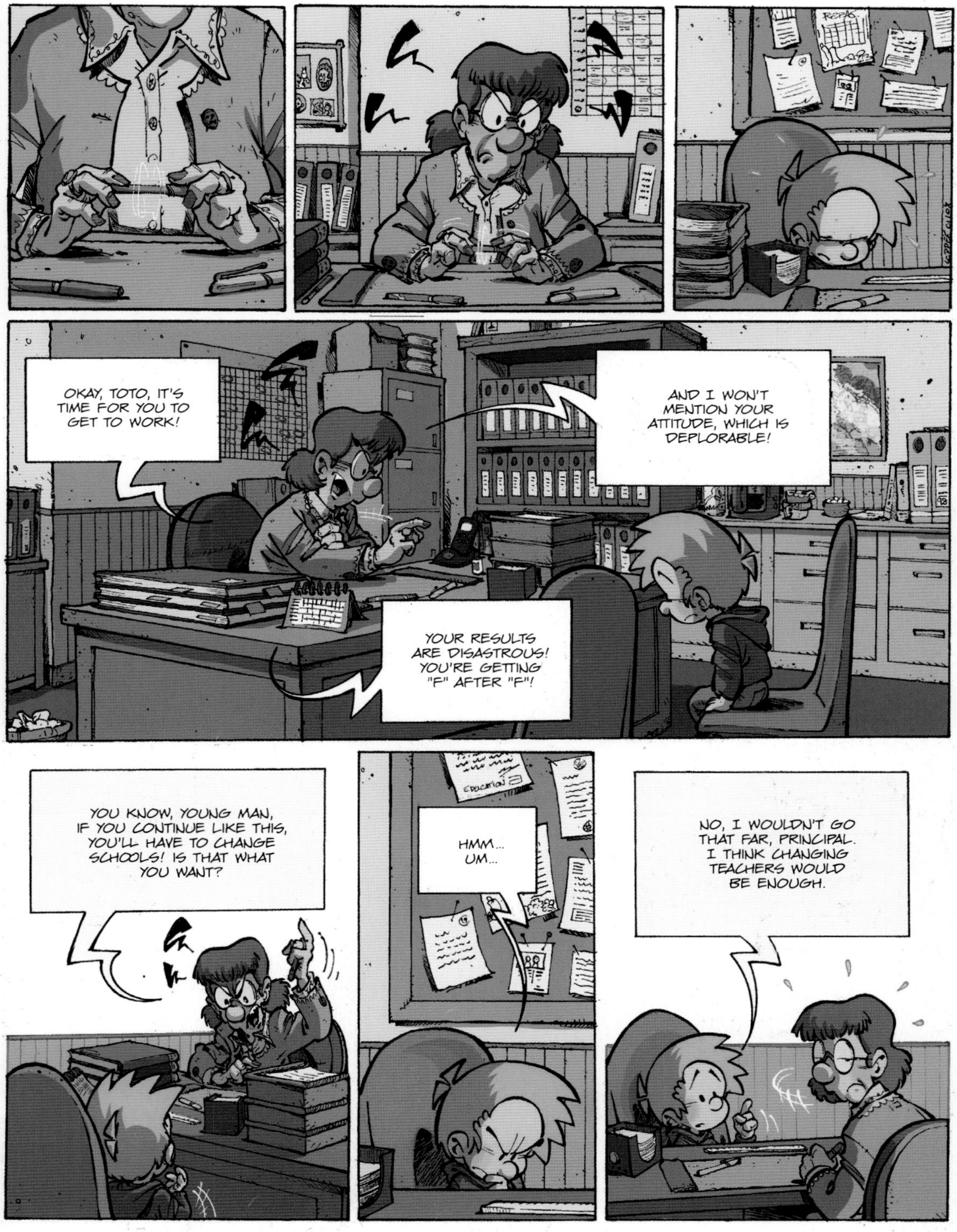
OKAY, TOTO, IT'S TIME FOR YOU TO GET TO WORK!
AND I WON'T MENTION YOUR ATTITUDE, WHICH IS DEPLORABLE!
YOUR RESULTS ARE DISASTROUS! YOU'RE GETTING "F" AFTER "F"!
YOU KNOW, YOUNG MAN, IF YOU CONTINUE LIKE THIS, YOU'LL HAVE TO CHANGE SCHOOLS! IS THAT WHAT YOU WANT?
HMM... UM...
NO, I WOULDN'T GO THAT FAR, PRINCIPAL. I THINK CHANGING TEACHERS WOULD BE ENOUGH.

Pizza Portioning

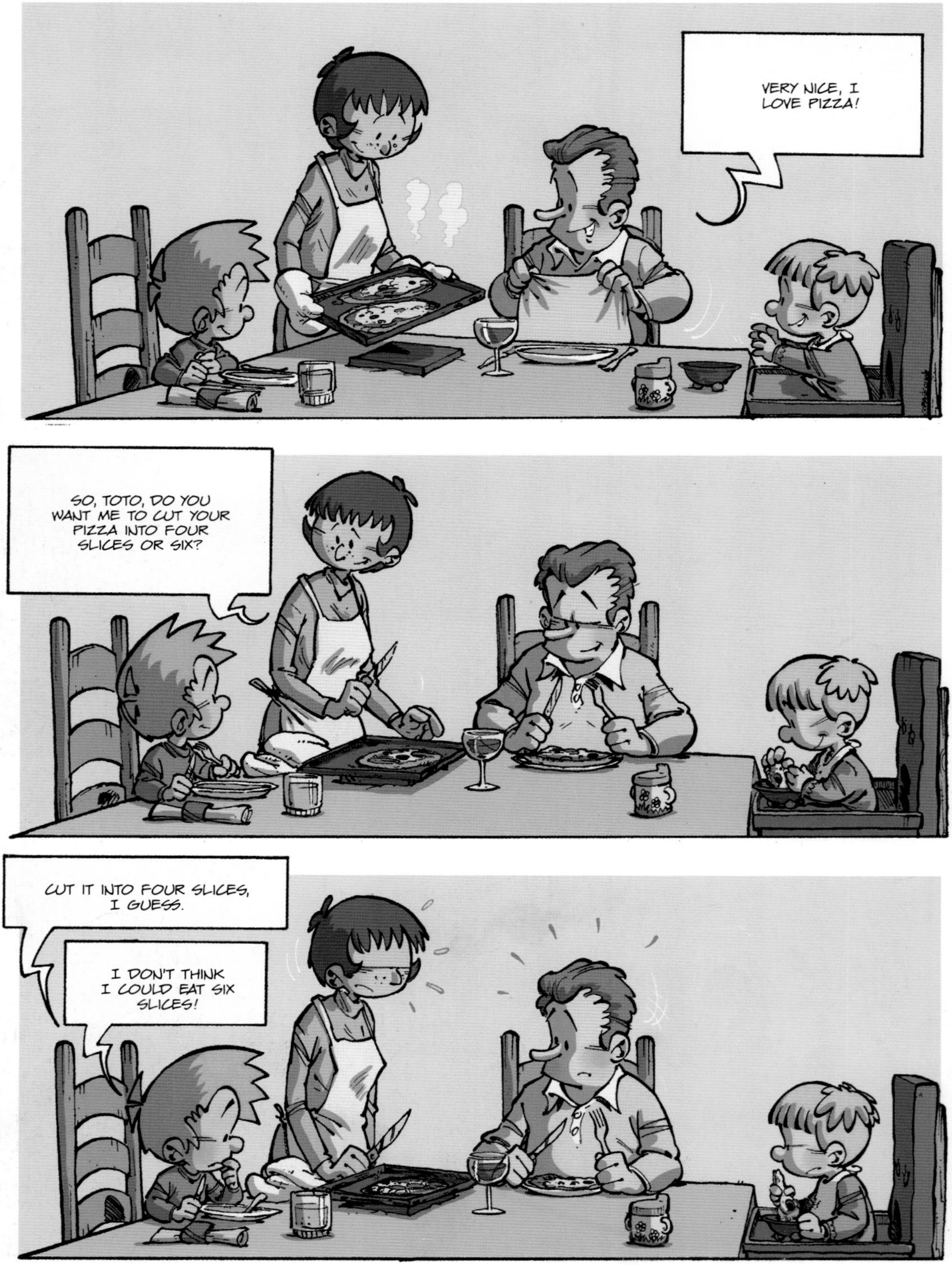

VERY NICE, I LOVE PIZZA!
SO, TOTO, DO YOU WANT ME TO CUT YOUR PIZZA INTO FOUR SLICES OR SIX?
CUT IT INTO FOUR SLICES, I GUESS.
I DON'T THINK I COULD EAT SIX SLICES!

The Addition Champion

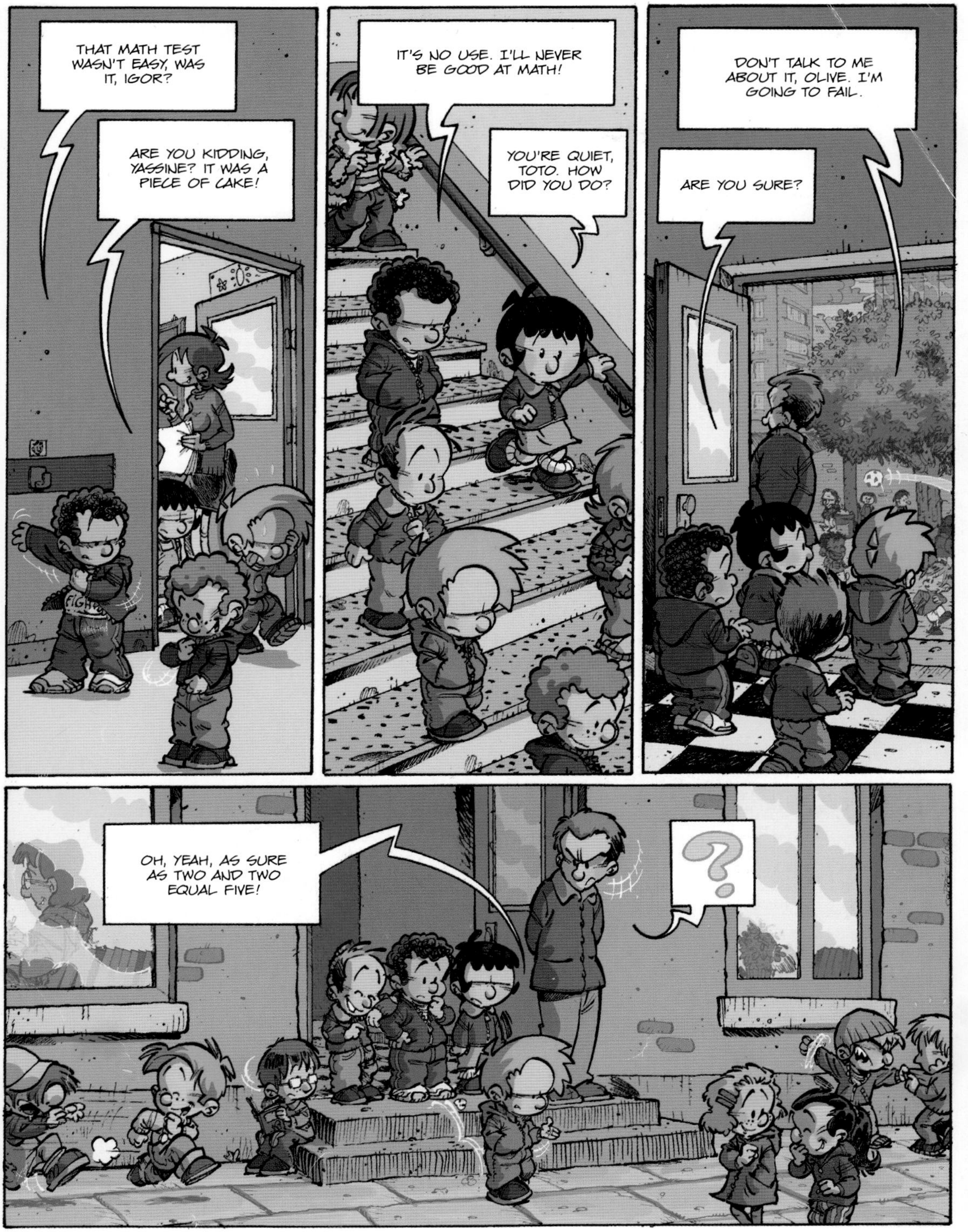
THAT MATH TEST WASN'T EASY, WAS IT, IGOR?
ARE YOU KIDDING, YASSINE? IT WAS A PIECE OF CAKE!
IT'S NO USE. I'LL NEVER BE GOOD AT MATH!
YOU'RE QUIET, TOTO. HOW DID YOU DO?
DON'T TALK TO ME ABOUT IT, OLIVE. I'M GOING TO FAIL.
ARE YOU SURE?
OH, YEAH, AS SURE AS TWO AND TWO EQUAL FIVE!
?

Day of the Dish

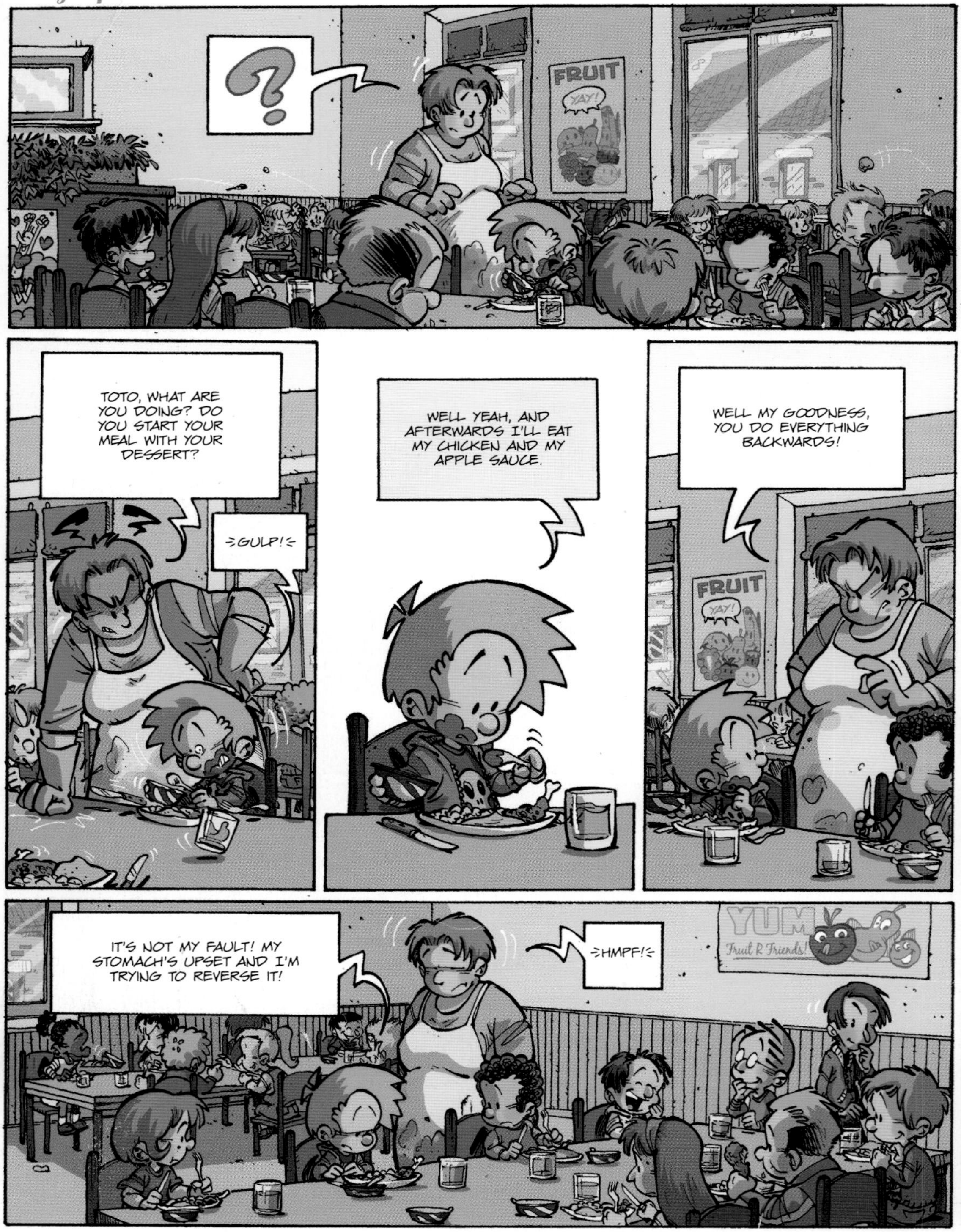
?
TOTO, WHAT ARE YOU DOING? DO YOU START YOUR MEAL WITH YOUR DESSERT?
GULP!
WELL YEAH, AND AFTERWARDS I'LL EAT MY CHICKEN AND MY APPLE SAUCE.
WELL MY GOODNESS, YOU DO EVERYTHING BACKWARDS!
FRUIT
YAY!
IT'S NOT MY FAULT! MY STOMACH'S UPSET AND I'M TRYING TO REVERSE IT!
HMPF!
YUM
Fruit R Friends!

Beating Around the Bush

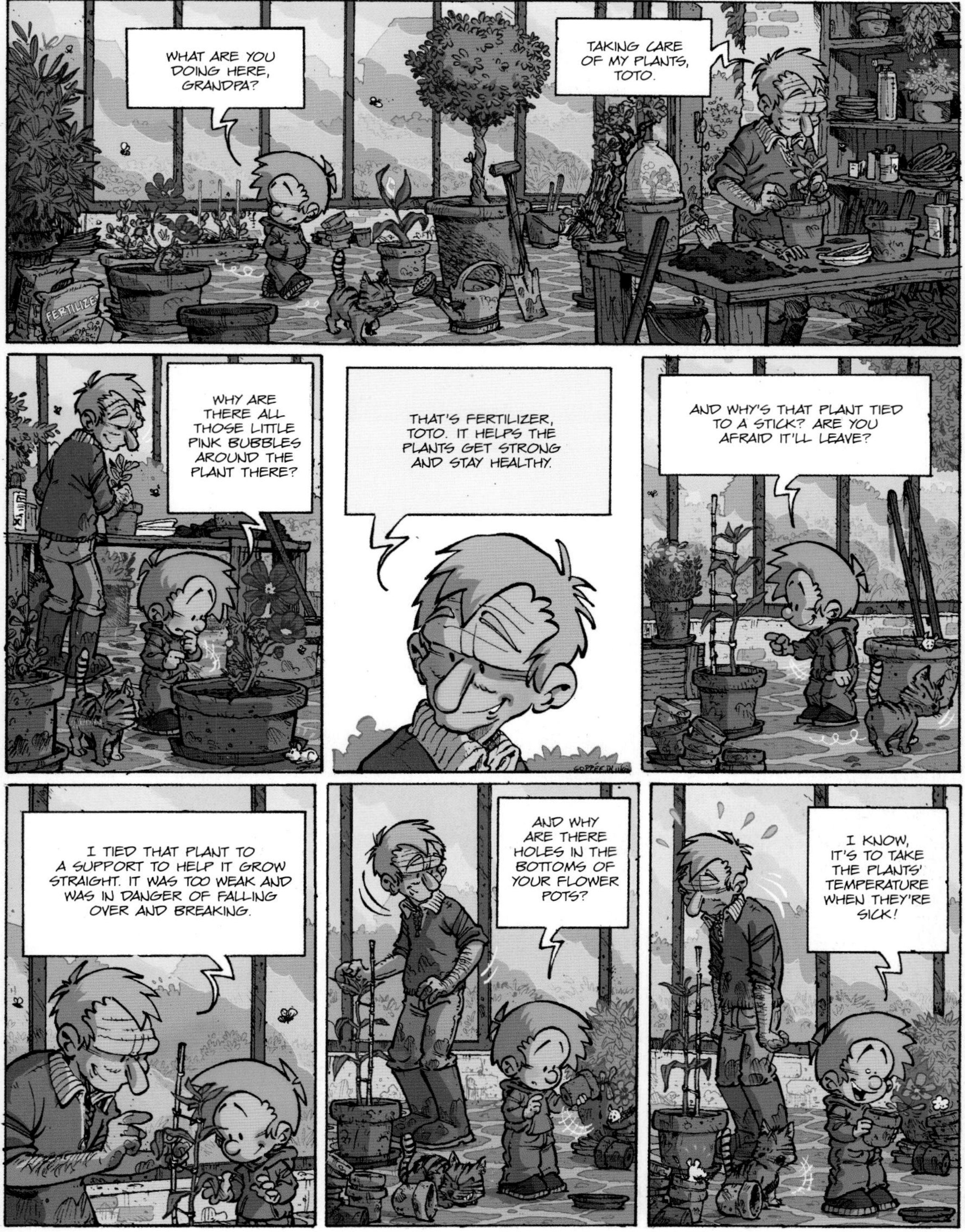

WHAT ARE YOU DOING HERE, GRANDPA?
TAKING CARE OF MY PLANTS, TOTO.
WHY ARE THERE ALL THOSE LITTLE PINK BUBBLES AROUND THE PLANT THERE?
THAT'S FERTILIZER, TOTO. IT HELPS THE PLANTS GET STRONG AND STAY HEALTHY.
AND WHY'S THAT PLANT TIED TO A STICK? ARE YOU AFRAID IT'LL LEAVE?
I TIED THAT PLANT TO A SUPPORT TO HELP IT GROW STRAIGHT. IT WAS TOO WEAK AND WAS IN DANGER OF FALLING OVER AND BREAKING.
AND WHY ARE THERE HOLES IN THE BOTTOMS OF YOUR FLOWER POTS?
I KNOW, IT'S TO TAKE THE PLANTS' TEMPERATURE WHEN THEY'RE SICK!

Caught at all Cost

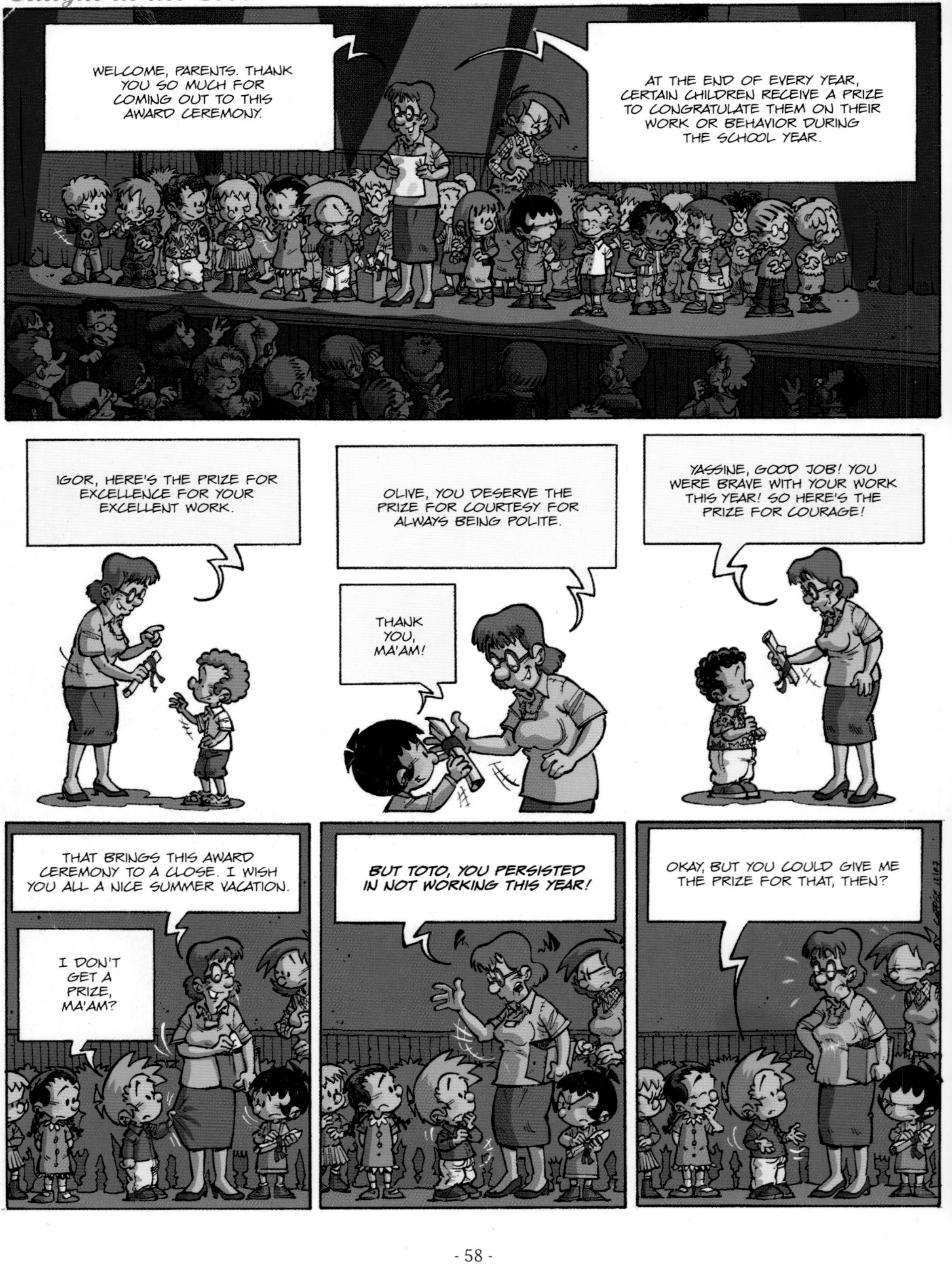
WELCOME, PARENTS. THANK YOU SO MUCH FOR COMING OUT TO THIS AWARD CEREMONY.
AT THE END OF EVERY YEAR, CERTAIN CHILDREN RECEIVE A PRIZE TO CONGRATULATE THEM ON THEIR WORK OR BEHAVIOR DURING THE SCHOOL YEAR.
IGOR, HERE'S THE PRIZE FOR EXCELLENCE FOR YOUR EXCELLENT WORK.
OLIVE, YOU DESERVE THE PRIZE FOR COURTESY FOR ALWAYS BEING POLITE.
THANK YOU, MA'AM!
YASSINE, GOOD JOB! YOU WERE BRAVE WITH YOUR WORK THIS YEAR! SO HERE'S THE PRIZE FOR COURAGE!
THAT BRINGS THIS AWARD CEREMONY TO A CLOSE. I WISH YOU ALL A NICE SUMMER VACATION.
I DON'T GET A PRIZE, MA'AM?
BUT TOTO, YOU PERSISTED IN NOT WORKING THIS YEAR!
OKAY, BUT YOU COULD GIVE ME THE PRIZE FOR THAT, THEN?

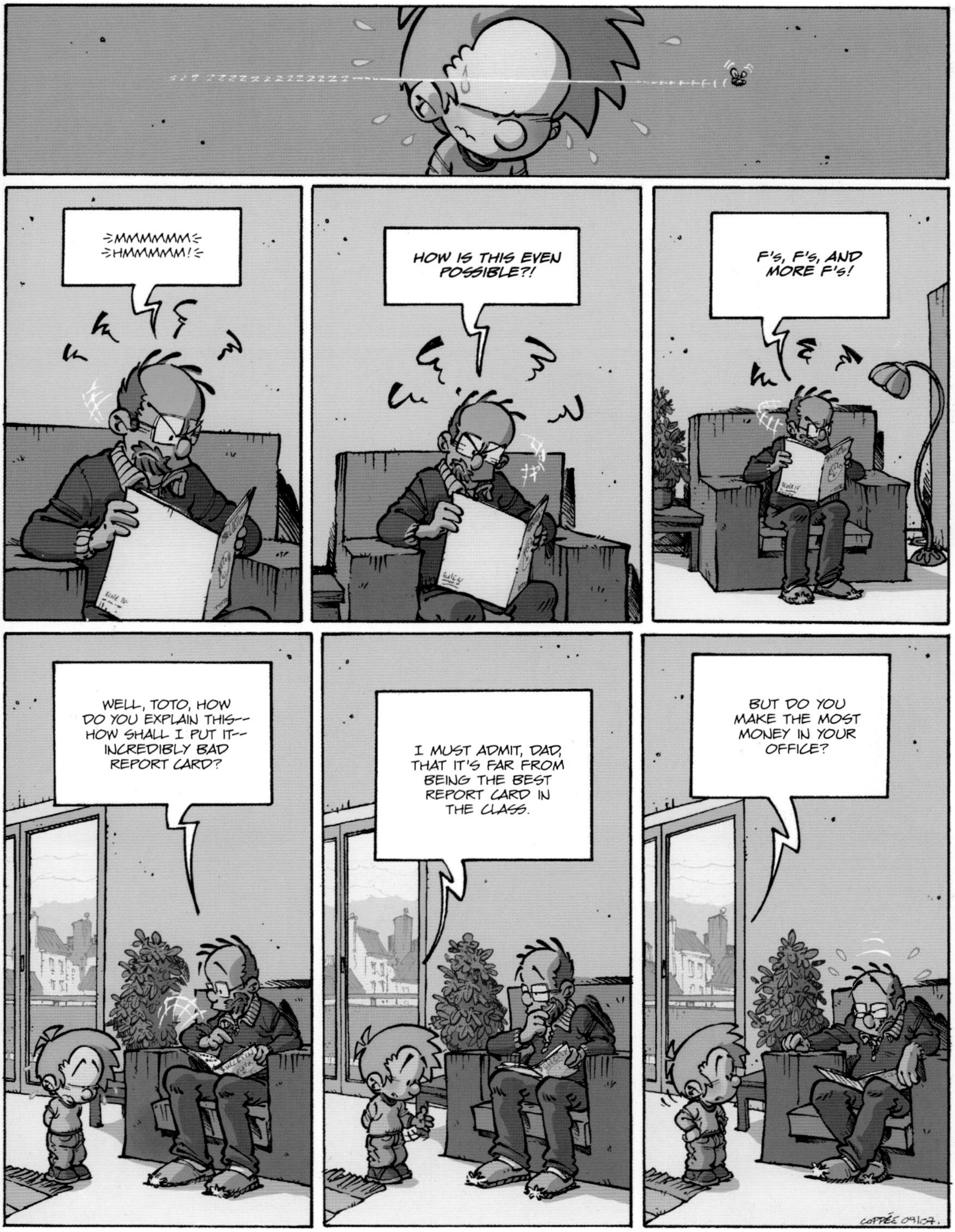
ZZZ ZZZZZZZZZZZZZ
=MMMMMM=
=HMMMMM!=
HOW IS THIS EVEN POSSIBLE?!
F's, F's, AND MORE F's!
WELL, TOTO, HOW DO YOU EXPLAIN THIS-- HOW SHALL I PUT IT-- INCREDIBLY BAD REPORT CARD?
I MUST ADMIT, DAD, THAT IT'S FAR FROM BEING THE BEST REPORT CARD IN THE CLASS.
BUT DO YOU MAKE THE MOST MONEY IN YOUR OFFICE?
COPPÉE 09/07.

Calculus of Love

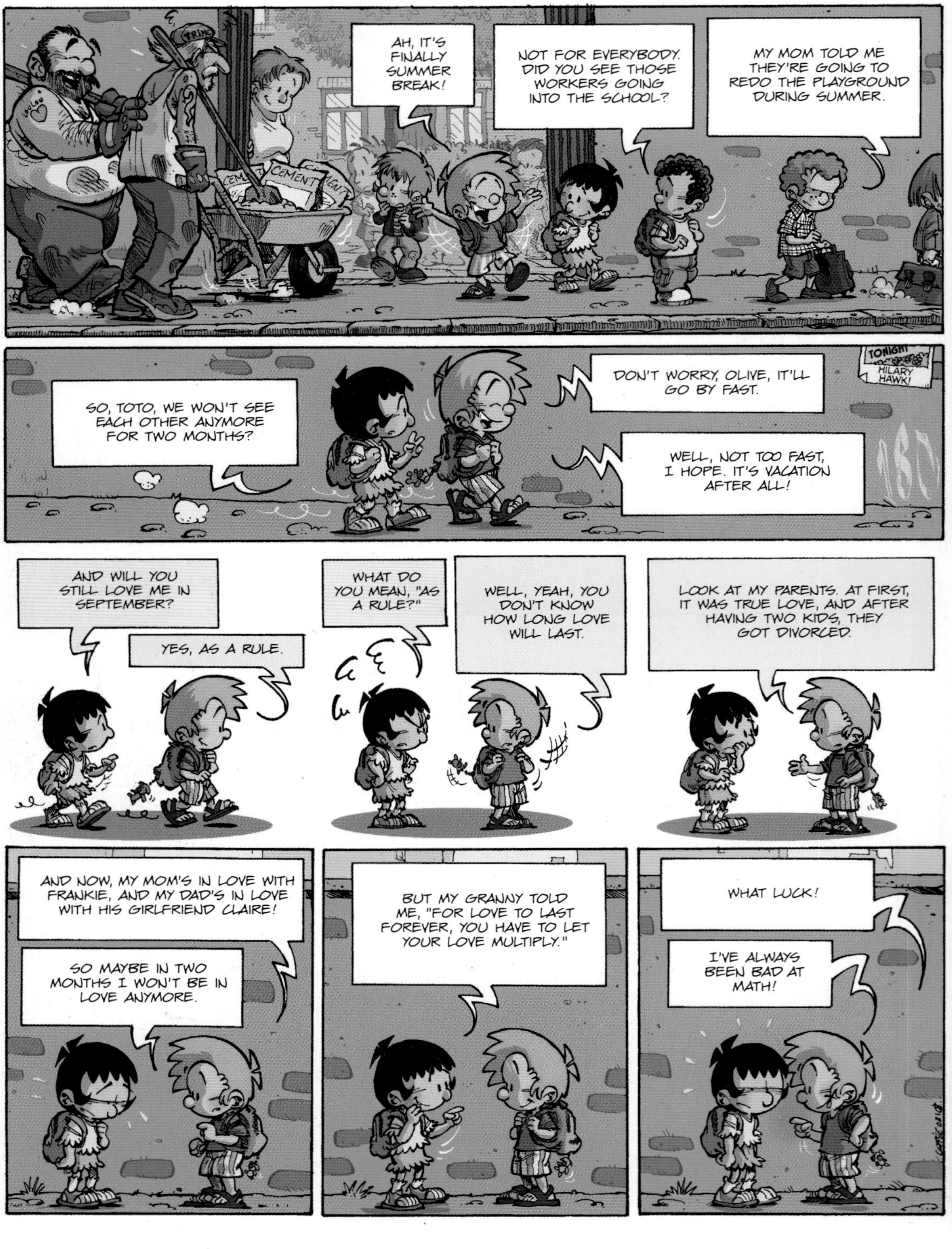

CEMENT
CEMENT
AH, IT'S FINALLY SUMMER BREAK!
NOT FOR EVERYBODY. DID YOU SEE THOSE WORKERS GOING INTO THE SCHOOL?
MY MOM TOLD ME THEY'RE GOING TO REDO THE PLAYGROUND DURING SUMMER.
TONIGHT HILARY HAWK!
SO, TOTO, WE WON'T SEE EACH OTHER ANYMORE FOR TWO MONTHS?
DON'T WORRY, OLIVE, IT'LL GO BY FAST.
WELL, NOT TOO FAST, I HOPE. IT'S VACATION AFTER ALL!
AND WILL YOU STILL LOVE ME IN SEPTEMBER?
YES, AS A RULE.
WHAT DO YOU MEAN, "AS A RULE?"
WELL, YEAH, YOU DON'T KNOW HOW LONG LOVE WILL LAST.
LOOK AT MY PARENTS. AT FIRST, IT WAS TRUE LOVE, AND AFTER HAVING TWO KIDS, THEY GOT DIVORCED.
AND NOW, MY MOM'S IN LOVE WITH FRANKIE, AND MY DAD'S IN LOVE WITH HIS GIRLFRIEND CLAIRE!
SO MAYBE IN TWO MONTHS I WON'T BE IN LOVE ANYMORE.
BUT MY GRANNY TOLD ME, "FOR LOVE TO LAST FOREVER, YOU HAVE TO LET YOUR LOVE MULTIPLY."
WHAT LUCK!
I'VE ALWAYS BEEN BAD AT MATH!

Strawberry Sundaze

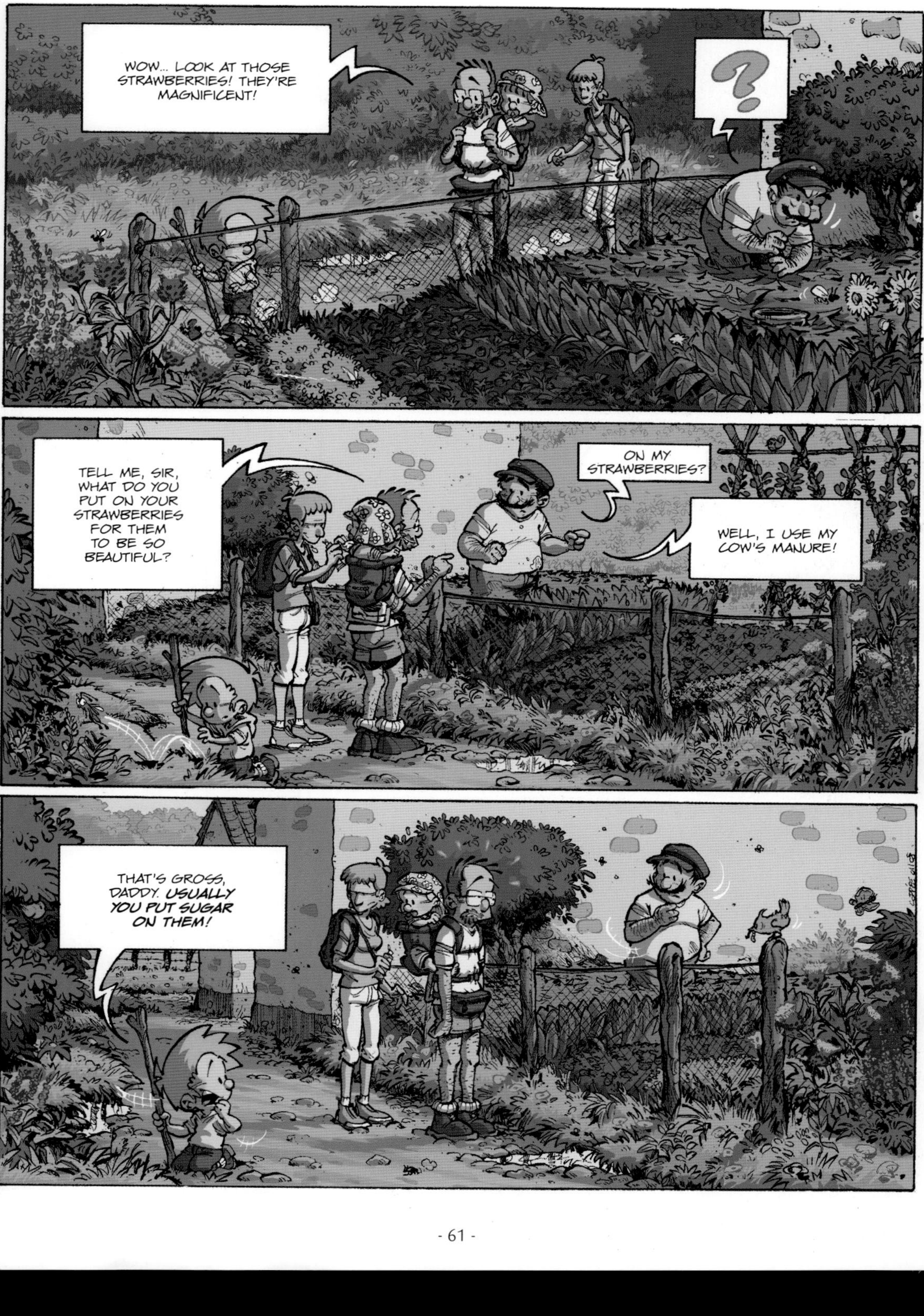
WOW... LOOK AT THOSE STRAWBERRIES! THEY'RE MAGNIFICENT!
?
TELL ME, SIR, WHAT DO YOU PUT ON YOUR STRAWBERRIES FOR THEM TO BE SO BEAUTIFUL?
ON MY STRAWBERRIES?
WELL, I USE MY COW'S MANURE!
THAT'S GROSS, DADDY. *USUALLY YOU PUT SUGAR ON THEM!*

Fish Tales

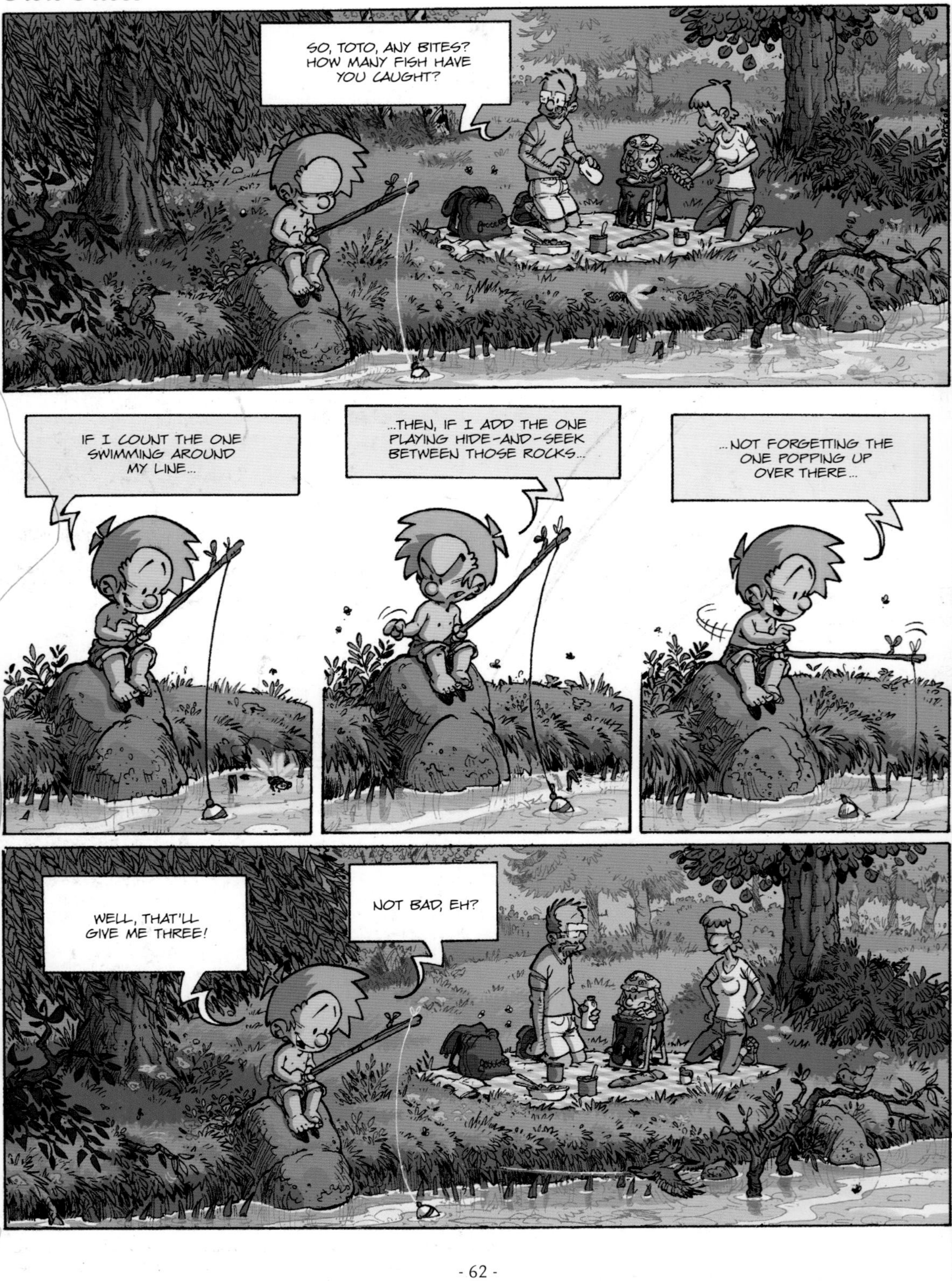
SO, TOTO, ANY BITES? HOW MANY FISH HAVE YOU CAUGHT?
IF I COUNT THE ONE SWIMMING AROUND MY LINE...
...THEN, IF I ADD THE ONE PLAYING HIDE-AND-SEEK BETWEEN THOSE ROCKS...
...NOT FORGETTING THE ONE POPPING UP OVER THERE...
WELL, THAT'LL GIVE ME THREE!
NOT BAD, EH?

WATCH OUT FOR PAPERCUTZ™

Welcome to the tasteless, tact-free, teacher-unfriendly, temerarious and tenacious third TOTO TROUBLE graphic novel by Thierry Coppée from Papercutz, the teeny-tiny company that's dedicated to publishing great graphic novels for all ages. I'm Jim Salicrup, your tardy Editor-in-Chief and part-time teacher's pet, here to come clean, and make a candid confession…

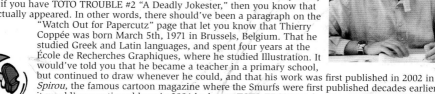

Thierry Copeé

As Lou Costello, the chubby half of an old comedy team, would often lament, "I'm a baaaad boy." In TOTO TROUBLE #1's "Watch Out for Papercutz" page, I promised that TOTO TROUBLE #2 would feature a short biography and a photo of the very talented and very funny Thiery Coppée. And if you have TOTO TROUBLE #2 "A Deadly Jokester," then you know that no such bio or pic actually appeared. In other words, there should've been a paragraph on the "Watch Out for Papercutz" page that let you know that Thierry Coppée was born March 5th, 1971 in Brussels, Belgium. That he studied Greek and Latin languages, and spent four years at the École de Recherches Graphiques, where he studied Illustration. It would've told you that he became a teacher in a primary school, but continued to draw whenever he could, and that his work was first published in 2002 in *Spirou*, the famous cartoon magazine where the Smurfs were first published decades earlier. And it would've mentioned how in 2004 he began TOTO TROUBLE (or *"Les Blagues de Toto"* as it is known in French) for the world-famous graphic novel publisher Delcourt. I hope you (and Thierry Coppée) can forgive me for not including all that wonderful information in TOTO TROUBLE #2 "A Deadly Jokester." Maybe one day in the future, we'll be able to finally publish that biographical information here in TOTO TROUBLE. But until then, I offer my sincere apologies.

BENNY BREAKIRON

Speaking of bad boys, what we did mention in TOTO TROUBLE #2 was a bunch of other Papercutz titles featuring kids (and one donkey) that embrace the somewhat wild side of childhood. We mentioned Tom Sawyer, who appears in two adaptations of the Mark Twain tale in CLASSICS ILLUSTRATED DELUXE #4 and CLASSICS ILLUSTRATED #19, both published by Papercutz. We happily talked about BENNY BREAKIRON, the super-strong French boy who starred in his own Papercutz graphic novel series, but will soon be featured in THE SMURFS AND FRIENDS graphic novels from Papercutz. We explained who ARIOL is, and highly recommended his ongoing Papercutz graphic novel series, and we rhapsodized about a six-and-a-half year-old girl and her best friend, who happens to be a microbe, and who both star in the ERNEST & REBECCA graphic

DENNIS THE MENACE

ERNEST & REBECCA

novel series from Papercutz. But now we're proud to announce that Papercutz will soon be publishing comics' original bad boy, DENNIS THE MENACE! Years ago, Hank Ketchum created a nationally syndicated comic strip character inspired by his own son—Dennis the Menace. It was so insanely popular that soon there was a hit TV series based on Dennis, which lead to countless imitations. Marvel Comics, for example, published PETER THE LITTLE PEST. But fortunately, there was an authorized DENNIS THE MENACE comicbook series, and many comics critics and historians, not to mention comics fans and cartoonists, consider that series a true achievement in comic art. Especially the work of Owen Fitzgerald and the team of Fred Toole and Al Wiseman. These fans have been waiting for a comics publisher to finally collect these classic comics in a format worthy of such great comics, and we're happy to announce, that's exactly what we're planning to do!

It all comes down to the fact that Papercutz is, like we always say, truly dedicated to publishing great comics for all ages. Whether it's classic comics such as DENNIS THE MENACE or BENNY BREAKIRON or brand new works of comics art such as ERNEST & REBECCA, ARIOL, or TOTO TROUBLE, we're just interested in finding the very best written, most beautifully drawn, and absolutely the funniest comics in the world, and bringing them to you to enjoy!

ARIOL

Thanks,

Jim

STAY IN TOUCH!

EMAIL: salicrup@papercutz.com
WEB: papercutz.com
TWITTER: @papercutzgn
FACEBOOK: PAPERCUTZGRAPHICNOVELS
MAIL: Papercutz, 160 Broadway, Suite 700, East Wing, New York, NY 10038

More Great Graphic Novels from PAPERCUTZ

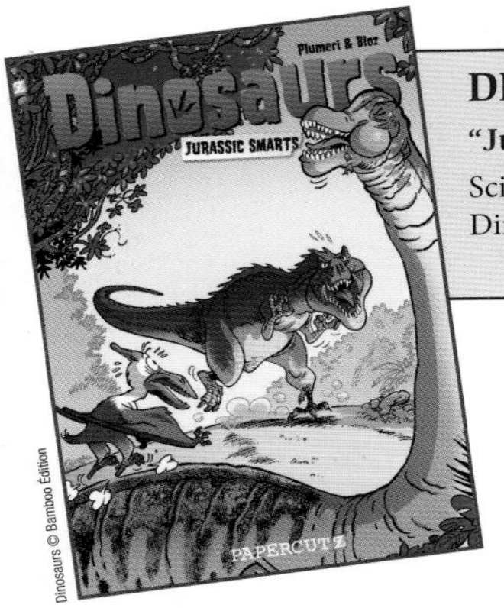

Plumeri & Bloz
Dinosaurs
JURASSIC SMARTS
PAPERCUTZ

DINOSAURS #3
"Jurassic Smarts"
Science facts combined with Dino-humor!

ERNEST & REBECCA #5
"The School of Nonsense"
A 6 ½ year old girl and her micro-bial buddy against the world!

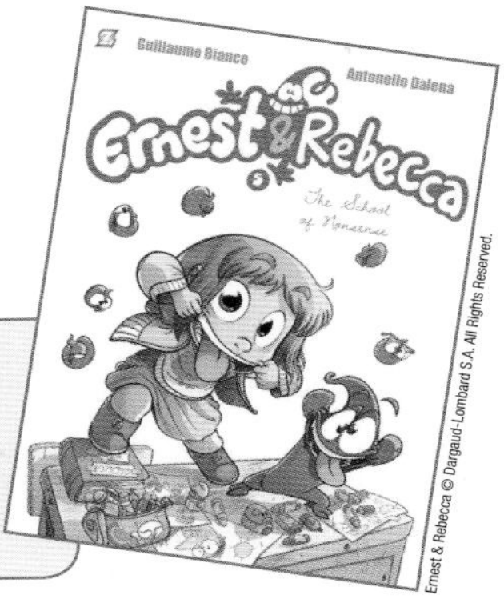

Guillaume Bianco
Antonello Dalena
Ernest & Rebecca
The School of Nonsense

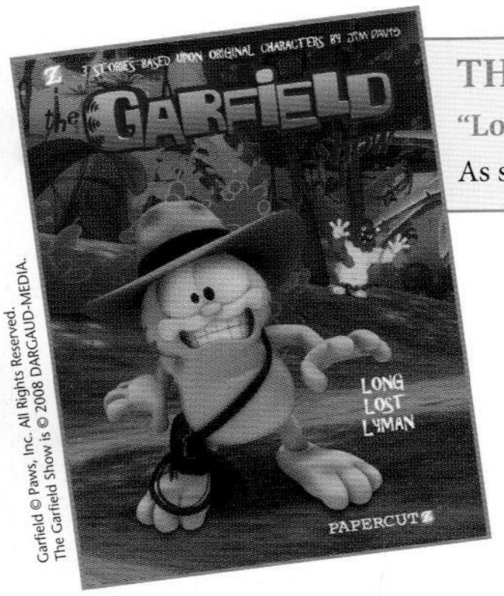

7 STORIES BASED UPON ORIGINAL CHARACTERS BY JIM DAVIS
the GARFIELD
LONG LOST LYMAN
PAPERCUTZ

THE GARFIELD SHOW #3
"Long Lost Lyman"
As seen on the Cartoon Network!

BENNY BREAKIRON #4
"Uncle Placid"
Benny helps his Uncle protect the finance minister of Fürengrootsbadenschtein from all kinds of dangerous danger!

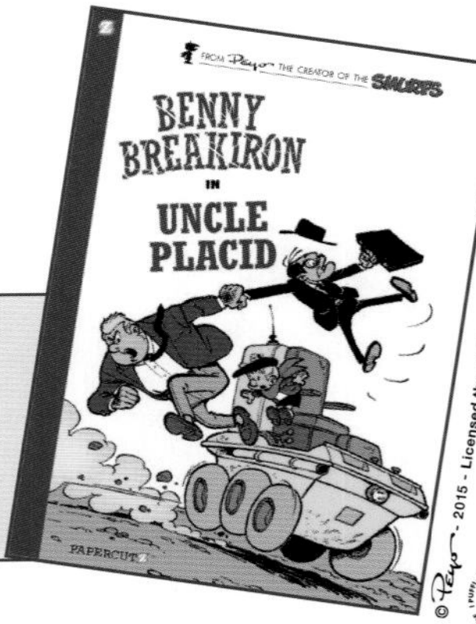

FROM Peyo THE CREATOR OF THE SMURFS
BENNY BREAKIRON
IN
UNCLE PLACID
PAPERCUTZ

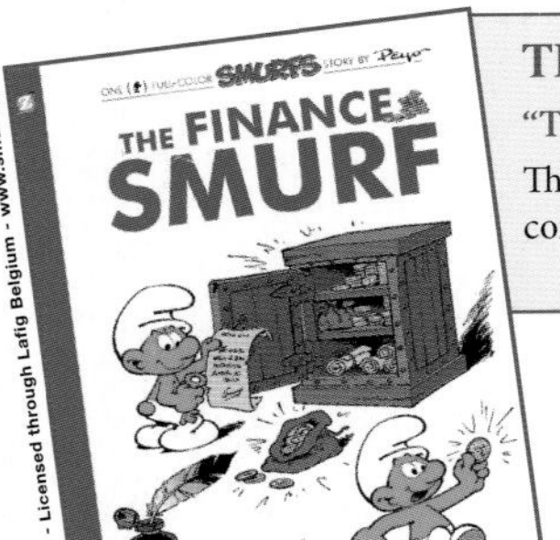

SMURFS
THE FINANCE SMURF
PAPERCUTZ

THE SMURFS #18
"The Finance Smurf"
The Smurfs learn that with money comes problems!

LEGO® LEGENDS OF CHIMA #4
"The Power of Fire CHI"
Laval must harness the power of CHI to fend of the ice-hunter tribes!

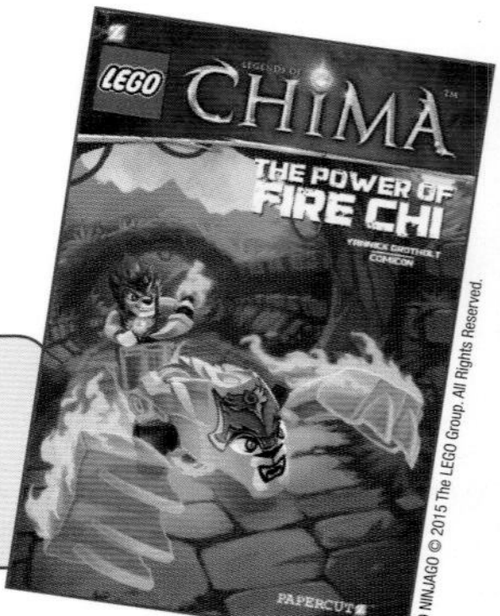

LEGO
CHIMA
THE POWER OF FIRE CHI
PAPERCUTZ

Available at better booksellers everywhere!

Or order directly from us! DINOSAURS is available in hardcover only for $10.99; ERNEST & REBECCA is $11.99 in hardcover only; THE GARFIELD SHOW is available in paperback for $7.99, in hardcover for $11.99; BENNY BREAKIRON is available in hardcover only for $11.99; THE SMURFS are available in paperback for $5.99, in hardcover for $10.99; and LEGO LEGENDS OF CHIMA is available in paperback for $7.99 and hardcover for $12.99.

Please add $4.00 for postage and handling for the first book, add $1.00 for each additional book.

Please make check payable to NBM Publishing. Send to: PAPERCUTZ, 160 Broadway, Suite 700, East Wing, New York, NY 10038
(1-800-886-1223)

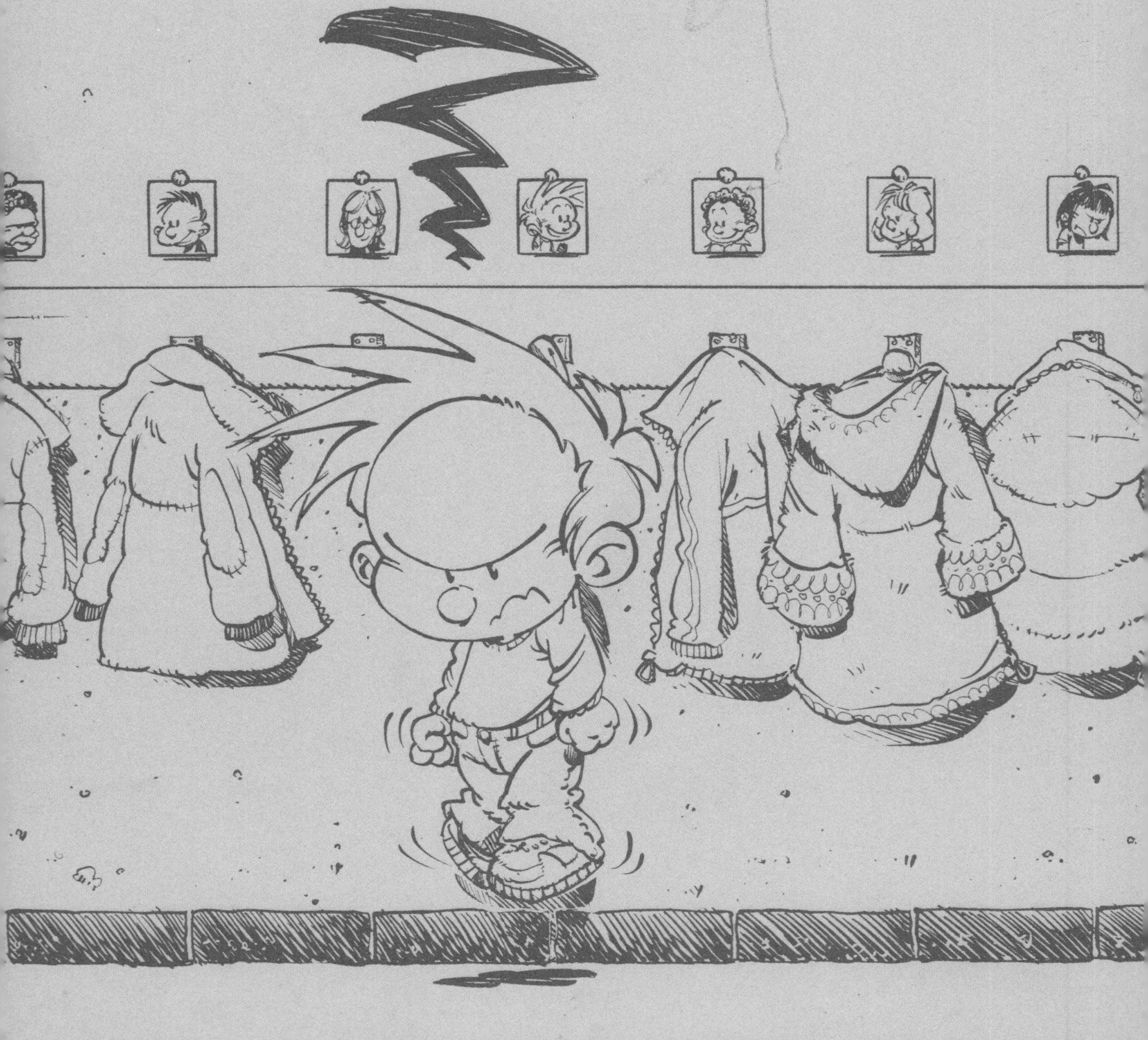